ABOUT THE ALDEN ALL STARS

Nothing's more important to Derrick, Matt, Josh, and Jesse than their team, the Alden Panthers. Whether the sport is football, hockey, baseball, or track and field, the four seventh-graders can always be found practicing, sweating, and giving their all. Sometimes the Panthers are on their way to a winning season, and sometimes the team can't do anything right. But no matter what, you can be sure the Alden All Stars are playing to win.

"This fast-paced [series] is sure to be a hit with young readers."   —*Publishers Weekly*

"Packed with play-by-play action and snappy dialogue, the text adeptly captures the seventh-grade sports scene."   —*ALA Booklist*

The *Alden All Stars* series:

ALDEN ALL STARS

Wild Pitch

David Halecroft

Ethan

PUFFIN BOOKS

PUFFIN BOOKS
Published by the Penguin Group
Viking Penguin, a division of Penguin Books USA Inc.,
375 Hudson Street, New York, New York 10014, U.S.A.
Penguin Books Ltd, 27 Wrights Lane, London W8 5TZ, England
Penguin Books Australia Ltd, Ringwood, Victoria, Australia
Penguin Books Canada Ltd, 2801 John Street, Markham, Ontario, Canada L3R 1B4
Penguin Books (N.Z.) Ltd, 182–190 Wairau Road, Auckland 10, New Zealand

Penguin Books Ltd, Registered Offices: Harmondsworth, Middlesex, England

First published in Puffin Books, 1991
1   3   5   7   9   10   8   6   4   2
Copyright © Daniel Weiss Associates, Inc., 1991
All rights reserved
The author also writes as "Joe M. Hudson"

Library of Congress Catalog Card Number: 90-50837
ISBN 0-14-034548-5

Printed in the United States of America
Set in Century Schoolbook

Wild Pitch

1

If there was one thing Jesse Kissler knew how to do, it was throw a fastball.

"Let's see some speed, Jesse," Derrick Larson cried, crouching behind the plate and lifting his catcher's mitt. "Fire it right down the pipe."

Eddie Peres stood at the plate, near the old wooden fence in Jesse's backyard. The spring sun, blazing down on the town of Cranbrook, felt hot on his neck. It was the beginning of baseball weather, and the three friends were getting ready for the season.

Eddie cocked the bat. Jesse wound up, pitched, and the fastball sped right toward Derrick's mitt. Eddie took a big cut, keeping his head level. A solid *crack!* rang out in the spring air.

Jesse's jaw dropped. He spun around and watched the ball sail all the way across his backyard, over the apple trees, and straight toward the big plate-glass window in the dining room.

"Oh, no!" Jesse cried, his eyes frozen wide open.

"Curve, curve!" Derrick Larson called out, yanking the catcher's mask away from his face.

"Miss the window!" Eddie Peres shouted, still holding the bat. "Please, miss the window!"

At the last second, the ball curved and hit the bricks, barely three inches from the window. It bounced off the house and landed with a splash in the birdbath.

"Home run!" Eddie shouted. He dropped the bat and lifted his arms in triumph. "Right into the birdbath. Now that's luck!"

"Just be glad you didn't break the window!" Jesse exclaimed with relief. He took off across the lawn to retrieve the ball.

Jesse was a tall, lanky boy, whose arms and legs seemed a little too long for his body. When Jesse ran, he sometimes looked like he was going to get all tangled up in his own feet. But what Jesse lacked in speed around the bases, he made up for with his blazing fastball. He had been the best pitcher on the Cranbrook Little League team, and had led the squad to victory in the league championships.

Now the boys had left Fairwood Elementary School, and entered Alden Junior High. Little League was behind them, and the first practice for seventh grade baseball was the next day. Compared to Little League, it seemed like "real" baseball. Jesse was a little nervous about pitching in junior high. All the other players were bigger, and the games were seven innings long. He hoped his fastball would be good enough to get him through.

He picked the wet ball out of the birdbath, and wiped it off on his pants. Then he ran back toward Eddie and Derrick.

"That was a close call," Jesse said, underhanding the ball to Eddie.

"It's two days worth of good luck if you hit a ball into water," Eddie said as he bare-handed Jesse's throw.

"But it would have been a whole season of bad luck if we'd broken the window," Jesse answered.

"I wish you guys would lay off that superstition stuff," Derrick said, putting his catcher's mask back on. Derrick's hair was so blond it looked almost white. His blue eyes glinted between the bars of the mask. He had just moved to Cranbrook from Minnesota that fall, so Derrick's accent still sounded funny to the Cranbrook boys. "You don't really believe all that good luck and bad luck stuff, do you?"

Jesse and Eddie shrugged, but didn't say a word.

During the summer, Jesse had read an article about the superstitions of big league pitchers. Some of them wouldn't even go out to the mound unless they had a special good luck charm with them. Jesse started putting his baseball card of Roger Clemens—the great Red Sox starter—in the band of his baseball cap as his own good luck charm. He even covered the card with plastic so it wouldn't get soggy from sweat.

Pretty soon, Eddie had become interested in superstition, too. It had all started out as a big joke, but as time went on the two boys began to believe more and more in good luck and bad luck. Without his good luck card, Jesse was sure he wouldn't be able to pitch a single strike.

Derrick didn't think any of it made sense.

"I can't believe you really go for that stuff," Derrick said, shaking his head. "You're going to need more than just good luck to play junior high ball."

"Junior high baseball won't be any problem," Eddie said with a shrug. "Not for the Alden Panthers."

"I hear the hitters will be better in seventh grade," Jesse said. "And the pitchers, too."

"You've got the fastest fastball in the league," Eddie answered. "No one will be able to beat you."

"And with Eddie at shortstop," Derrick added, "no grounders will ever slip out of the infield."

Eddie had played shortstop all through Little League, and he wanted to keep playing shortstop on the seventh grade team. In fact, Eddie's good luck charm was a special white T-shirt autographed by Luis Rivera—his favorite shortstop. Every time he went out to play baseball, Eddie wore that T-shirt underneath his uniform.

"Watch out!" someone shouted from the yard next door to Jesse's.

The three boys looked up in time to see a baseball fly over the fence. It landed with a thud a few feet away.

A tall boy came into the yard and ran toward the ball. "Sorry about that," he said.

It was Nick Wilkerson, Jesse's next door neighbor, followed by Nick's friend Sam. Nick was in eighth grade at Alden Junior High. Ever since Jesse was a little boy, he had looked up to Nick Wilkerson. Nick was only a year older than Jesse, but he seemed to know everything—the right way to tie knots, fix a broken radio, and even the right way to pitch a baseball or slam a homer.

"Nick really got ahold of that one," Sam said, picking up the ball. "I gave him a nice easy pitch and he creamed it all the way over here."

"If Jesse were pitching, I bet Nick wouldn't be able to *touch* the ball," Eddie said. "Jesse's fastball is *hot*."

"Okay, Mr. Fastball," Nick said, picking up the bat and smiling. He walked over to the plate and tapped his cleats. "Let's see if you're ready to pitch in junior high."

"Okay," Jesse said. He felt his heart begin to pound inside his chest. There was nobody in the world Jesse wanted to strike out more than Nick Wilkerson.

"Hey, are you and Eddie still superstitious?" Nick said, taking some practice swings.

Jesse blushed a little and shrugged.

"Okay, then," Nick continued. "What would happen if I hit your best pitch through your bedroom window?"

"That would be bad luck for Jesse," Eddie answered. "Probably a whole season of bad luck."

Jesse nodded, but he wasn't too worried about Nick. There was no way in the world anyone could hit a fastball that far. Besides, the bedroom window wasn't a very big target.

"Give me your best fastball," Nick said. Derrick crouched down behind him to catch. Nick cocked the bat back, flexed his knees, and stared right into Jesse's eyes.

I'll show him what my fastball is all about, Jesse thought. He reached up to his cap and touched the baseball card. Then he licked his fingertips, wiped them on his pants, and gripped the ball, laying two fingers right along the seams. He went into his windup, dropping his foot back and turning on the grass. He kept his eyes on the target that Derrick made with his catcher's mitt.

Jesse wanted to pitch a blazing fastball right down the middle. He had a nice long stride in his delivery, and got all of his strength behind the throw. When he released the ball, he knew that the pitch was perfect. He watched the ball speed right toward Derrick's mitt.

Nick took a big, easy swing. Jesse heard the crack of the bat, and felt his spirits sag. He turned around and watched the ball sail high above the apple trees,

over his mother's flower garden, across the patio—
right toward his bedroom window high on the second
floor.

"Wow, check it out! Amazing!" Everyone was
shouting behind him. But Jesse didn't say a word.
He just stood and watched.

Crash!

He heard the sound of broken glass smashing on
the patio below. Jesse turned as white as a ghost.
Behind him, the other four boys were speechless.
Finally Nick walked up to Jesse.

"I'm sorry," Nick said. "I never thought I'd *really*
break your bedroom window."

"It's okay," Jesse said, without even looking at
Nick.

"You don't believe in all that stuff about a season
of bad luck, do you?" Nick asked.

"You hit my best pitch for a home run," Jesse
pointed out. "And so did Eddie. That's not very good."

"Maybe Coach Lanigan will teach you some other
pitches, like the curve and the changeup," Nick
added. He and Sam turned to leave. "When you learn
those, I'm sure you'll do great."

Jesse just shrugged.

"Good luck at practice tomorrow," Nick called out
as he left the yard.

"He'll need it," Eddie muttered under his breath. Eddie touched the collar of his T-shirt, just so none of Jesse's bad luck would rub off on him.

"I guess we should go home," Derrick said, picking up his catcher's mask.

Eddie slung his bat over his shoulder. "See you tomorrow. I hope your mom isn't too mad about the window," he said before hurrying off.

Jesse said good-bye to his friends and walked slowly toward his house. He looked up and saw the jagged hole in his bedroom window. Of course, his mother would have something to say about that. But it was all the bad luck that really had Jesse worried.

2

"Dig, Jesse, dig!" Coach Lanigan shouted the next day at practice. "Round first and head to second!"

The Alden Panthers were doing their first real drill of the season. Each player had to run the bases as fast as he could. Jesse and Eddie were the last two runners, and the rest of the team was cheering them on from home plate. Jesse had started out way ahead of Eddie, but Eddie was catching up with every step.

"Pick up your heels, Jesse," Coach called. "Cut your corners sharp!"

On the baseline between second and third, Eddie caught up to Jesse and left him in a cloud of dust. He sprinted easily down the third-base line, and tucked his leg under for a beautiful slide into home. A few seconds later, Jesse puffed down the baseline and crossed the plate, all red in the face.

"Good hustle," Eddie said, slapping Jesse on the shoulder.

"I'm not as fast as you," Jesse replied, giving Eddie a high five. "But pitchers don't have to be fast."

Coach Lanigan called the boys to attention.

"I'm glad to see all that hustle out there," Coach began, as the team gathered around. He was a husky man with black hair and a deep voice. He went around to each player in turn, giving pointers on that day's practice. He came to Jesse last.

"Jesse, you need to cut your corners more sharply. If you don't, you'll lose time getting to the next base. Sloppy baserunning can cost us runs."

Jesse nodded. "I'll work on my baserunning, Coach. Maybe I'll even start passing Eddie on the baseline."

The whole team laughed, including Coach Lanigan. Everyone knew that Jesse would never be a great runner.

"I like this team's attitude," Coach said, making a few marks on his clipboard. "You guys have fun, but you also work hard. In baseball, it's the team with the best attitude that wins. I want everyone to remember that this year. Understand?" Everyone nodded. "Okay, let's do some fielding drills."

Coach looked down at his clipboard and called off names. Six players spread out on the infield, and six spread across the outfield.

Jesse jogged out to second base, and watched Coach dump a bag of balls in the dirt. Eddie had never really liked fielding.

Coach smacked the first grounder to Eddie at shortstop. Eddie charged the ball and kept his glove low. The grounder hit a pebble and took a bad hop, but Eddie was right there to block it with his chest. He snatched the ball from the dirt and whipped it to Derrick at home plate.

"Great play, Eddie," Coach said, picking up another ball. "Did everyone see how Eddie charged the ball and kept his body in front? That's heads-up fielding."

The next grounder came speeding right toward Jesse. He backed up, spread his legs, and put his

12

glove down. The next thing he knew, the ball had slipped between his legs and rolled out to center field.

"Jesse, you need to charge the ball," Coach said. "You also need to keep your knees bent and your glove down."

Coach picked up another ball and smacked a hard grounder to Dan Folger, at third base. Dan bobbled the ball once, then got control and hurled it to Derrick. Rich Roberts looked like a good infielder, too, and so did J. P. Schweitzer at first base. But every time a grounder came to Jesse, it rolled right between his legs.

"What's wrong out there, Jesse?" Coach said, after Jesse missed another.

"I'm a pitcher, Coach," Jesse answered, with an embarrassed smile. "Not a second baseman."

"All players need to field well," Coach said. "Even pitchers." After hitting a few more grounders he gave the bat to Dan, and called out to the field, "Everyone who's interested in pitching, come over to the sidelines. Everyone else, keep working on fielding."

Coach told Dan to hit flies and grounders to the rest of the team. Derrick put on his catcher's pads. Only Jesse and Matt Kindel walked over to the sidelines with Coach.

13

"Are you the only two interested in pitching?" Coach said, rubbing his chin. "We're going to need more than two pitchers. We need at least two starting pitchers and one relief pitcher."

"Eddie has a good arm," Jesse said, pointing to the infield where Eddie was shagging grounders. "But he wants to play shortstop."

"That's okay," Coach said. "He can still play shortstop and be a relief pitcher." He put his hands around his mouth and called Eddie from the infield. Eddie ran over, and stood next to Jesse and Coach.

"Jesse tells me you have a good arm," Coach said.

Eddie glanced at Jesse, then shrugged.

"How would you like to try pitching?" Coach asked. "We need more than just two pitchers."

"Well I was hoping to . . . ," Eddie began.

"I know, you want to play shortstop," Coach said. "If you're a relief pitcher, you can play both positions."

"Okay," Eddie nodded, after a pause. He seemed uncertain about the idea of pitching, but Jesse gave him a smile and a little thumbs-up. If Eddie became a pitcher, then Eddie and Derrick and Jesse would get to spend a lot of time together at practice.

"Let me tell you something about the game of baseball," Coach said, tossing a ball up and down in one hand. "Baseball is seventy-five percent pitching. If you have great pitching, you'll win baseball games, no matter what. But pitching is the hardest thing to do in baseball. A lot of boys your age think that pitching is just throwing the ball as hard as you can. Now don't get me wrong, speed and power are important in pitching. But so is control. You've got to be able to work the batter. Understand?"

The three boys nodded.

"Okay," Coach went on. "Each of you take turns pitching to Derrick. Ten pitches each, then rotate."

Matt pitched first. He was a medium-sized boy, and he had always been the second-string pitcher on Jesse's Little League team. He was a good pitcher, although he walked too many batters.

Coach stood behind Derrick and watched Matt pitch, checking out his form. He threw a pitch in the dirt, and Derrick made a great save, falling onto his knees in front of the ball and blocking it with his chest pad.

"That's the stuff, Derrick," Coach said. "A catcher can't be afraid of the ball."

Eddie was next on the mound. He had a nice, slow, controlled motion. He was small and his pitches weren't fast, but they were usually in the strike zone.

After ten pitches, Jesse walked up to the mound

and took the ball in his hand. He touched the Roger Clemens baseball card in his cap for good luck, licked his fingers, and wiped them off on his pants. He gazed straight at Derrick's target, and then began his windup. He released the ball, and it raced toward Derrick's target.

There was a loud *smack* when the ball hit Derrick's mitt.

"Ouch!" Derrick said, taking off his mitt and shaking his hand. "That's like catching a bullet."

"Great pitch, Jesse," Coach said, impressed. "Try another one. This time pitch it low and inside."

Derrick held his glove low and inside, and Jesse hurled the ball right on target. Most of his pitches were as fast and good as his first one.

"Go ahead and throw another ten, Jesse," Coach said.

As Jesse pitched, a little smile spread across Coach's face. When Jesse had finished, Coach blew his whistle and told everyone to gather for batting practice. He put a player in each position on the field to catch any hits.

"Jesse, I want you on the mound," Coach said, tossing him a new ball.

Jesse caught the ball, nodded, and tried not to

break into a big, silly grin. This was his chance to
show Coach what he could really do.

The first batter up was Dan Folger. Jesse touched
the baseball card in his cap, licked his fingers, and
wiped them on his pants. He sent Dan a fastball right
down the center of the plate. Dan took a big cut, and
missed.

"Strike one!" Coach said.

The next pitch was exactly the same—super-fast
and right down the middle. Dan took another big cut
and missed.

"Keep your eye on the ball," Coach told Dan. "Follow it all the way into your bat."

The third pitch was another fastball—but this
time Dan was ready for it. He took a big swing, but
only got a little piece of the ball. It bounced to Eddie
at shortstop. Eddie gathered it in and chucked it to
first for an out.

"Good pitching, Jesse," Eddie said, as the boys
threw the ball around the horn. "Now strike the next
one out."

The next batter was John Lilly. John was one of
the biggest boys on the team, and one of the best
hitters. He had a funny batting stance—crouched
way down low. But Jesse wasn't intimidated. He

threw three perfect fastballs, right down the middle. John swung and missed all three.

"You're out," Coach said, lifting his thumb.

Jesse struck out the next four batters, too. It seemed like no one could get a piece of Jesse's blazing fastball. Coach Lanigan leaned up against the backstop with his arms crossed and watched Jesse pitch.

"Good practice, men," Coach said later, as the team headed off to the locker room. "Jesse, you pitched great today. If we all work hard, this team can have a fine season."

Jesse was psyched after practice that day.

"Nick was right," Jesse said. He and Eddie and Derrick were heading to the Cranbrook Mall for a soda. "I didn't get bad luck just because he hit my pitch and broke my bedroom window. I think I got good luck instead."

"Your fastball sure was looking hot today," Derrick said.

"Hey, speaking of fastballs," Eddie said, tapping Jesse on the shoulder. "Why did you volunteer me to be a pitcher?"

"If you pitch, then the three of us will be able to hang out all practice long."

"That's true," Eddie nodded, smiling. "It might be fun to be a relief pitcher."

"Don't worry," Jesse said, taking off his cap and pulling the Roger Clemens card from it. He waved it in front of his two friends. "You won't have to do much relief pitching when *I'm* on the mound."

3

Jesse's pitch went right down the pipe, speeding like a comet. Bruce Judge started to swing but by the time his bat had come around, Jesse's fastball had shot past him, right into Derrick's mitt.

"Strike three!" Coach Lanigan called.

Bruce chucked his bat into the dirt and tossed his batting helmet to the next Panther batter, Eddie Peres.

"Keep smoking, Jesse," the infielders chattered,

as Eddie stepped up to the plate. "Give this guy the heat!"

It was the second week of practice and the Panthers were playing their first scrimmage game. Coach Lanigan had announced everyone's position the day before. Derrick was catcher, Rich Roberts was second baseman, Dan Folger was third baseman, and J. P. Schweitzer was at first. Eddie was shortstop, and also relief pitcher. Matt Kindel was second-string pitcher, and left fielder. John Lilly was in center field, and Zack Herschel was covering right field.

Jesse was starting pitcher.

It was only the second inning, and Jesse had struck out three of the last five batters. The other two had dribbled easy ground balls, both of them right into the first baseman's glove.

Now Eddie was at the plate, with two down and no one on base.

Jesse touched the card in his cap, licked his fingers, and wiped them off on his pants. He played with the ball in his glove, until he found the seams, and laid his two fingers right across them. He always pitched the two-finger fastball, using the seams to get extra speed and control. He wound up and pitched.

Crack!

Eddie sent the ball floating high above the infield, deep into left center. Matt had been playing Eddie shallow. Now he had to turn around and run so fast that his cap blew off his head. He held his glove out in front of him, made a last ditch leap—and snagged the ball as he slid across the grass. He lifted his glove above his head and waved the ball to show everyone.

"Great catch, Matt," Coach Lanigan called, as the two teams traded sides. "And Eddie, that was a great hit. You really read Jesse's pitch."

Jesse and Eddie gave each other a high five as they changed sides.

Eddie was pitching for the other team, and he hadn't given up any runs, either. Jesse had been watching Eddie's style from the bench, and he thought he had Eddie figured out. When Jesse stepped up to the plate—with two outs and no one on base—he was sure he could hit whatever Eddie threw him.

Eddie wound up and pitched. The ball came in fast and low. Jesse took a huge cut and felt the solid part of the bat hit the ball. He followed through on his swing and sent the ball sailing high above the second baseman's head.

"Go, Jesse, go!" Coach called.

Jesse dropped the bat and took off toward first. As he ran, he watched the ball soar above Zack's head in right field and drop to the ground. Jesse wasn't the fastest runner on the team, but he decided to round first and try for a double anyway. He didn't cut his corner very sharply, though, and almost ended up running in the grass of the outfield. Rich Roberts hurried to second base and put his glove up for Zack's throw.

It was going to be a close play at second, and Jesse knew it. He pumped his arms as hard as he could and kept his eyes focused on the white base. If he had to, he'd try to take out Rich with his slide, and make him drop the ball.

Zack's throw was right on the money. Jesse even heard the ball slapping into Rich's glove. He tucked his right leg under his body and dropped to the dirt for the slide. Rich dropped his glove for the tag.

"Out!" Coach called. "Great hit, Jesse, but not so great baserunning. You didn't cut your corner sharp enough."

Jesse was mad at himself for being slow. Still, it felt so great to smack the ball out to center field that he couldn't help smiling as he ran back to the bench.

Next inning the first batter Jesse faced was John Lilly. John was the Panthers' best hitter, and he strolled confidently out to the plate. He crouched down in his strange, low batting stance and gazed right into Jesse's eyes.

I'm going to blow this fastball by you, Jesse thought, touching his good luck card.

He started his windup and chucked the ball right down the middle.

Crack!

Jesse watched the ball sail deep into left field and drop before Matt could reach it. John rounded first and headed for second. Matt's throw sailed over the second baseman, and landed in foul territory. It was Jesse's job to get the loose ball, and he took off for it.

"Come on, come on!" Coach called to John, making a big windmill with his arm. "Go for third!"

John rounded second. Jesse finally got the ball, bare-handed it and made an off-balance throw to Dan Folger at third. It was a great throw, but a split second too late. John slid right beneath Dan's tag.

"Safe!" Coach Lanigan called. "Great hit, and great running, John!"

Jesse was a little flustered. He wondered how John could have hit one of his best pitches, and decided to try throwing faster than usual. He walked the next two batters.

"Don't throw too hard, Jesse," Coach called out. "You lose your control."

Suddenly, the bases were loaded with no outs. Even though it was a cool spring day, Jesse was sweating. He slowed his next pitch down. The batter stroked it for an easy single, batting in two runs.

The inning didn't end until Jesse had given up four runs, and lost the scrimmage. Practice was over.

"Jesse, Eddie, Matt, Derrick," Coach called out, as the Panthers walked across the grass toward the locker rooms. "Can you stay behind for a few minutes?"

The four boys walked over and stood in front of Coach.

"Listen," Coach said to Jesse, Matt, and Eddie. "You all have the makings of good pitchers. But you have to learn to vary your pitches. Otherwise, you're going to throw your arms out. Boys your age get injured when they throw too many fastballs." Coach smiled and tossed Jesse a ball. "Also, the batters will be able to figure out what you're doing. After an inning or two of strikeouts, they're going to start popping hits. Just like today."

"I'll just throw harder and faster," Jesse said.

"Then you'll have problems with control," Coach said. "I think you need to learn some new pitches—

maybe the curve and the changeup. I want to make sure you have new pitches for our first game next week, against Bradley."

"That sounds great!" Jesse, Matt, and Eddie said together.

Derrick gave his friends a smile, and put his catcher's equipment back on. Coach Lanigan tossed one ball to Jesse, one to Matt, and one to Eddie.

"Now grip the ball just like a fastball, except more in the fingers," Coach said, showing them what he meant. "Besides that, the only difference between a fastball and a curveball is in the delivery. For a curveball, you snap your wrist down just before you throw. That puts a big spin on the ball, and the spin makes the ball curve right before it reaches the plate."

He made them try the motion a few times slowly, until they got it down.

"This is easy," Jesse said, running out to the mound. "Let me give it a try."

Derrick jogged over to the plate and squatted down.

Jesse gripped the ball just as Coach had shown him. He started his windup, kicked his leg, and made his delivery, snapping his wrist just as he released the ball.

The ball flew straight into the grass, skipping 10 feet to the left of Derrick.

He tried it another five or six times, and each time seemed a little better than the one before it. Still, he couldn't get his curveball into the strike zone.

"Eddie, you try a few," Coach said.

Jesse walked off the mound and flipped the ball to Eddie. Eddie wound up and pitched, snapping his wrist on the delivery. The ball didn't have much speed, but Jesse could see it break sharply to the right. Derrick had to lunge to catch it.

"That's good, Eddie," Coach said. "Try it again, but this time follow through more."

Eddie pitched again, and this time the throw was faster. It curved right into the strike zone. Every pitch Eddie threw was better than the one before it.

"You sure are picking this up quick," Coach said to Eddie. "Now I don't want you boys to throw too many curves until your arms get used to the motion."

Coach left the four boys with a bag of balls. Jesse watched for Coach to disappear. Then he told Derrick he wanted to work on a few more curves. He tried to make his curves look like Eddie's, but every time he pitched, the ball went skidding into the backstop.

"Ball four!" someone called out from beneath the pines.

It was Nick Wilkerson, walking home from eighth grade team practice with his bat slung across his shoulder. Jesse's face turned bright red.

"What's up?" Nick said, smiling.

"We're learning the curve," Jesse said, looking at the ground and tossing the ball in his glove.

"How's it going?" Nick asked.

"Eddie's getting it pretty quick," Jesse answered. "But I can't get mine into the strike zone."

"These pitches take a long time," Nick said. "Just remember to follow through on the pitch."

With that, Nick started off on his way home.

"Oh, by the way," Nick called out, turning around with a smile. "How's your luck holding out?"

"Fine, I guess," Jesse said with a shrug. "We'll see what happens in the game against Bradley next week."

That night, Jesse flopped down on his bed and looked at the broken window. His father had taped a piece of cardboard to the pane, so the cool air wouldn't come in. Jesse wondered why Eddie was pitching so much better than he was. Eddie wasn't even supposed to be a pitcher. Maybe his luck really was starting to go bad.

4

"Will you quit checking for that baseball card?"
Derrick said, smiling and elbowing Jesse in the ribs.
He was sitting next to Jesse on the bus ride to Bradley. They were wearing their game uniforms, with
the blue shirts, white pants, and gold socks. Every
few minutes, Jesse would take off his blue cap and
make sure his good luck baseball card was still stuck
in the band. "You're making me nervous," Derrick
added.

"You realize that if I lose that card, I'm sunk in

the game today," Jesse said. "You don't want that, do you?"

Derrick rolled his eyes. He was about to say something, but Coach Lanigan called the bus to attention.

"Listen up, men," Coach began, standing in the aisle. "Bradley has good hitting, so we're going to need to stay alert in the field. I want to hear some chatter for Jesse today because he's got a big job to do on the mound. But the best way we can support him is to put the bat on the ball and score some runs. Okay?"

The whole bus let out a big cheer. Jesse jumped to his feet, held up his finger, and got the whole team chanting, "Number one, number one, number one!"

The day was perfect for baseball—sunny, with big white clouds drifting in the blue sky. The field at Bradley looked great as well. The grass had just been cut, and the dirt on the infield had been raked. The bases were new, and very white against the deep brown dirt. They didn't stay white for long, though.

Jesse was batting in the number one position. As he walked toward the plate he took a deep breath and touched his special good luck card. He stepped into the batter's box, cocked the bat, and watched the pitcher wind up and deliver. The ball sped right toward the plate. Jesse decided to swing. He felt the ball hit the sweet spot of the bat, and take off over the pitcher's head.

A hit!

The fly ball dropped toward shallow center field. The Bradley fielder made a long, diving leap. He didn't make the catch, but he trapped the ball beneath his body. Jesse saw the fielder rise to his knees with the ball in his hand. Jesse tried to make his long legs go as fast as they could. The center fielder whipped a great sidearm throw to first. The ball hit the first baseman's glove just as Jesse's foot hit the bag.

"Safe!" the umpire called. "Tie goes to the runner."

"Yes!" Jesse cried, trotting back to the base.

The pitcher must have been shaken up by Jesse's leadoff single, because he walked Rich Roberts in four pitches. Now there were men on first and second.

Derrick stepped up to the plate, and Jesse took a healthy lead off second base. If Derrick connected for a single, Jesse wanted to get a good jump on the ball and make it home for a run.

Jesse's heart skipped a beat when he heard the crack of Derrick's bat and saw the ball speed down the third-base line. From the corner of his eye, he saw the left fielder rush for the ball.

"Cut your corner sharp and head home!" Coach called out to Jesse. "Go, go!"

Jesse knew there'd be a play at the plate. When he cut around third base and headed for home, he saw the catcher flip off his mask and get into position for the throw.

"Slide, Jesse, slide!" Coach yelled.

Jesse didn't know why, but he decided to slide headfirst. He lunged forward, held out his arms, and hit the dirt. The catcher caught the throw, but Jesse hit him so hard that the ball flew out of his mitt and rolled toward the backstop. The catcher tumbled onto his back while Jesse slid across the plate on his stomach in a cloud of dust.

Jesse stood up immediately, and waved Rich Roberts home. Rich took advantage of the loose ball and sprinted down the third-base line. The Bradley catcher scrambled to get the ball. Rich made a slide just as the Bradley catcher was diving toward home with the ball in his bare fist. Rich touched the plate first. The two boys collided like two linebackers in a football game.

Rich was a little slow in getting up, but he was safe! All of a sudden, the Panthers had taken a two-run lead, and Derrick was safe at third with a stand-up triple.

The next three Panthers were retired in order, leaving Derrick stranded on third.

Still, it had been a great first inning of the season, and Jesse walked out to the mound feeling confident. He had worked hard on his curve and his changeup that week, and he wanted to test them out. Jesse and Derrick had also come up with their signals for pitches. If Derrick flashed one finger, that meant a fastball. Two fingers meant a changeup, and three meant a curve.

Before the first pitch, Coach joined Jesse on the mound. "I know you're nervous, but it's just first game jitters. I'm going to let you make your *own* decisions today. It will help you relax."

The first Bradley batter stepped up to the plate. Derrick flashed one finger. Fastball.

Jesse's heart was beating wildly. He touched his good luck card, then licked his fingers and wiped them on his pants. He started his windup—nice and slow—and then put his whole body behind the delivery.

The ball sped toward the strike zone. The batter swung and missed.

"Strike one!" the umpire called.

"Nice pitch, Jesse," Eddie called out behind him. "Throw it in there, c'mon, Jesse."

Next pitch, Derrick flashed three fingers for the curve.

I hope I can do it, Jesse thought. He touched his lucky card. Then he gripped the ball in his fingertips, went into his windup, and snapped his wrist down on the delivery. The ball sped toward the plate and broke sharply to the left. The Bradley batter took a swing and missed it by a mile.

"Yes!" Jesse cried. Derrick tossed the ball back and gave him a thumbs-up.

Derrick called for another curve, and Jesse pitched another beauty. The Bradley batter went down swinging, and Jesse chalked up his first official strikeout. He touched the Roger Clemens card again.

But things took a turn for the worse, anyway.

The next hitter was big, even bigger than John Lilly. If Jesse threw the wrong pitch, this guy could cream the ball. Derrick called for a curve. Jesse kept his eye on the catcher's mitt.

He knew it was going to be a bad pitch as soon as he released the ball—but he didn't think it would be *that* bad. The ball hit the grass and dribbled into the backstop for a wild pitch. The Bradley bench broke into laughter.

Jesse was more nervous than ever when Derrick called for another curveball. The same thing happened—another wild pitch that hit the dirt and bounced to the backstop. Jesse took a deep breath and tried not to listen to the jeers from the Bradley bench.

"There's a wild man on the mound," they cried, laughing.

Jesse breathed a sigh of relief when Derrick called for a fastball. He delivered a scorching pitch, but the Bradley batter swung and hit. It was a blazing grounder right toward Eddie at shortstop. Eddie backhanded it and chucked the ball to J. P. at first for the out.

Next, Derrick called for a changeup—and Jesse felt his heart begin to pound.

The changeup, at least, was a little easier to control than the curve. Jesse held the ball deep in his hand. He went over the pitch in his mind, remembering how to hold his wrist stiff in the delivery, to make the ball go very slow. If all went perfectly, the slowness of the changeup would throw off the batter's timing.

Jesse wound up and pitched. The ball floated way above the umpire's head for a wild pitch. Jesse felt his face burn with embarrassment and the Bradley bench continued their taunting. He hoped Derrick would call for a fastball next, but instead he called for a curve. Jesse threw another wild pitch. His confidence was destroyed.

Derrick called a curve again, but Jesse had had enough.

Forget it, Jesse thought. *I can't throw a curveball. I'm just going to stick with my fastball.*

Derrick kept calling for curves, but Jesse kept brushing off the signs and throwing fastballs. The Panther fielding came to the rescue, and Jesse got out of the inning without giving up a run.

"What's wrong?" Derrick asked Jesse, as they walked toward the bench. "How come you never pitch a curve when I tell you?"

"I was nervous," Jesse answered. "I'll throw the curves next inning."

Derrick kept calling for the curve and the change-up when the Bradley team was up at bat again, but Jesse only pitched him fastballs. Soon, the Bradley batters began to figure out that Jesse only had one pitch. Once they knew this, they began to time their swings.

It turned into a batter's game. Each team took their turns at the plate, knocking singles and doubles and driving in run after run. Bradley's brand-new bases got a lot of wear and tear. Luckily, Alden's bats were hotter than Bradley's. When the seventh inning ended, the score was Alden 14, Bradley 11.

The Panthers were cheering all the way home on the bus. Their hitting looked great, and their fielding had been solid—only two errors. Jesse was excited to have won his first game in junior high, and he gave everyone on the team high fives.

"Panthers rule!" they all shouted as the bus made its way back home toward Cranbrook. "Number one!"

Still, Jesse knew he hadn't pitched as well as he wanted to.

The bus dropped everyone off in the parking lot of Alden Junior High. Jesse, Derrick, and Eddie walked toward the locker room, carrying bags of bats and helmets and talking about the game.

"I hope Coach isn't mad at me for throwing so many fastballs," Jesse said.

"Why did you give up on your curve?" Derrick asked Jesse.

"I guess I need to work some more on it," Jesse answered. "I'll just stick with my fastball until I can get the others down."

"But it's not Little League anymore," Derrick answered. "The batters can figure out your pitches, like they did today. And you might hurt your arm."

Jesse just shrugged. "We won, didn't we?"

"We sure did!" Eddie smiled. He pulled up his base-ball shirt to show his good luck T-shirt underneath. "And it's all because of this," he added playfully.

"You wish," Jesse answered, laughing. He yanked off his cap, pulled out his good luck baseball card, and held it up in the air. "*This* is what made the Panthers win today."

Derrick shook his head and smiled.

5

The next day, Jesse and Derrick were tossing the ball around before practice and talking about their victory. A few eighth graders were strolling down to their field, carrying bases, batting helmets, and big green bags filled with bats.

"We can't let eleven runs be scored against us in every game," Derrick said, throwing a pop-up to Jesse. "And we can't always count on scoring fourteen runs ourselves."

"I know," Jesse answered, making the catch. "It was my fault that they scored so many runs."

"Your fastball was great," Derrick said. "Except when you tried to throw it too hard."

"A fastball is supposed to be fast," Jesse answered, whipping the ball straight into Derrick's mitt, where it made a loud smack.

"Ouch!" Derrick said, taking his mitt off and shaking his hand. "That's fast enough!"

"Nice throw!" came a voice from underneath the pine trees.

It was Nick Wilkerson, on his way to practice with the eighth graders. He had a bat slung across his shoulder. Jesse shouted hello and waved.

"Congratulations on your first junior high win," Nick said, walking over.

"Thanks," Jesse said, beaming with pride.

"I guess that broken window didn't end up being such bad luck after all," Nick teased.

Jesse's face turned a little red. "I guess not," he said. Then he reached up and touched the good luck baseball card in his cap.

"Let me take a cut at your best pitch," Nick said, tapping his cleats with his bat and stepping up to the plate. "Show me the stuff that beat Bradley."

"Okay," Jesse said, walking out to the mound. If

Jesse could ever strike Nick Wilkerson out, it would be the biggest strikeout of his life. It would mean he was really ready to pitch in junior high.

Derrick called for a curve, but Jesse decided to ignore it and pitch his fastball instead. If he screwed up his curve in front of Nick, he would be so embarrassed! Jesse wound up and sent the ball blistering over the middle of the plate.

Crack!

"Wow," Derrick said. He took off his catcher's mask and watched the ball sail all the way to the edge of the woods.

"I hate to say it, but I knew just where your pitch was going," Nick said to Jesse. "Your fastball is fast, but it always goes to the same place—and at the same speed. You've got to mix your pitches up." Nick picked up his glove and started jogging off the field. "I've got to get to practice. See you later."

All during practice, Jesse worked on his curves and changeups. He'd pitch ten balls, then Eddie and Matt would pitch ten. Eddie's curve was getting better and better with every practice, but Jesse tried not to let that bug him. Whenever he thought about how easy pitching came to Eddie, Jesse just got angry and lost his concentration.

It was Jesse's turn on the mound. Derrick called

for a changeup, and Jesse kept his wrist locked through the delivery—just like he was supposed to. The ball sailed over Derrick's head and into the backstop. Jesse kicked the dirt in frustration.

"Want to know what you're doing wrong?" Eddie asked. "You change your motion for each different pitch. It throws your timing off, and the ball goes everywhere."

"So what?" Jesse said, putting his hand on his hip. "You're not even a pitcher. I'm supposed to be the pitcher out here."

"I'm just trying to help," Eddie said.

"Well, maybe I don't need your help," Jesse answered. "I wish you'd stop trying to show me up all the time."

"I'm not trying to show you up," Eddie said. "And remember, you're the one who told Coach that I should pitch."

"Okay, okay," Derrick said, walking toward his friends. "We have work to do. We have to get Jesse's arm in shape for the Williamsport game."

Eddie gave Jesse a cool glance, then walked off the mound.

Sometimes, Jesse wished he had never volunteered Eddie to be a pitcher. Just thinking about it made him angry—and then his pitching got bad. So he took a deep breath and concentrated on hitting Derrick's catcher's mitt. By the end of practice, Jesse's curve was under control. It still wasn't as good as Eddie's, but at least he could get it into the strike zone.

On Friday, the Panthers played Williamsport at home.

"Keep your cool out there," Coach Lanigan told Jesse before the game. "That's the most important thing a pitcher can do. Williamsport has good pitching, and we're not going to be able to score as many runs as we did against Bradley. It's up to you to keep them from scoring." Coach gave Jesse an encouraging pat, and Jesse walked out to the mound.

Jesse's heart was racing in his chest. He took off his cap, glanced at his good luck baseball card, and took a deep breath. The first batter strolled up to the plate.

Derrick called for a curveball. Jesse felt a cold sweat break out on his forehead. He touched his baseball card, licked his fingers, and wiped them on his pants.

Throw it just like in practice yesterday, he told himself, starting his windup.

"And remember," Coach called. "Listen to your catcher."

Jesse snapped his wrist and the ball went sailing high above Derrick's head. Derrick leapt to his feet but the ball was way out of reach. Jesse turned around and kicked the rubber. He hoped Derrick would stop calling for curveballs—but Derrick called for a curve on the very next pitch.

When Jesse snapped his wrist this time, the ball flew right at the batter. The batter dropped to the dirt, but the ball hit him square in the shoulder.

"The batter was hit by the pitch," the umpire called out. "The batter gets first base."

"The pitcher can't pitch," the Williamsport boys called out from the bench. "If he keeps pitching like that, we'll all have to wear catcher's gear."

Jesse tried to ignore their jeers and concentrate on his pitching, but nothing seemed to go right. After walking the next two batters, he got so angry that he refused to throw any more curves or changeups. No matter what Derrick called for, Jesse decided to throw his fastball.

It was only the first inning, and already Jesse was in a jam. The bases were loaded, with only one down. The player at the plate was the Williamsport pitcher—a stocky boy, and a very slow runner. The infield was playing in a little, getting ready for a squeeze bunt. Since the bases were loaded, the Panthers could try a force-out at home plate.

Jesse wound up and pitched a fastball right across the plate. The batter turned toward Jesse and choked up on the bat. He connected! The ball dropped right down the third-base line for a perfect bunt.

Dan Folger charged in from third base, running neck and neck with the Williamsport runner who was speeding toward home. Derrick was standing on the plate, holding his catcher's mitt out for the force. Dan bare-handed the bunt and whipped it right past the runner's helmet and into Derrick's mitt for an out.

Derrick didn't lose an instant. He pulled the ball from his mitt and hurled it as fast as he could toward first base. The Williamsport pitcher was even slower than Jesse, and the ball beat him to the base by two full steps.

"They're both out!" the umpire called.

It was the most amazing double play Jesse had ever seen, and it couldn't have come at a better time.

In the second inning Jesse wasn't as lucky. Williamsport figured out Jesse's fastball and started to connect. When the top of the second was over, Williamsport had driven in three runs.

It was Alden's turn to rally. When Jesse left the on-deck circle, there were men at second and third, no outs. Jesse knocked the donut weight off his bat, adjusted his blue helmet, and stepped up to the plate.

If I can't pitch, at least I can hit, he thought.

Jesse tapped the plate and planted his feet. He gazed up at the pitcher, and cocked the bat behind his head. The very first pitch was a floater. Jesse took a big cut. His bat connected solidly with the ball. The Alden base runners took off while the hit dropped into shallow left field for an easy single.

Jesse rounded first, slowed, and saw the left fielder hurl the ball toward home. Zack sprinted toward the plate and slid—but the throw bounced under the catcher's legs and rolled toward the backstop. Jesse saw the loose ball and decided to go for second base.

"No, Jesse!" Coach called out. "Hold, hold!"

Jesse heard Coach too late. He stopped in the middle of the baseline just as the second baseman got the throw from the plate.

Jesse was in a rundown, trapped between first and second.

The second and first basemen began closing in on Jesse, and all Jesse could do was run back and forth, back and forth. Finally, he tried to make a mad dash back to first base. The second baseman flipped the ball to the first baseman, who tagged Jesse on the shoulder for an out.

Jesse's face was red as he ran back toward the bench. Still, he had driven home two runs, so everyone gave him high fives.

Those two runs were all that Alden scored that inning, bringing the score to Williamsport 3, Alden 2.

Jesse gave up a home run on his first pitch the next inning, and then two more hits right after. Suddenly there were men on first and third, with no outs. Derrick called for a changeup, and Jesse decided to give it one last try. The pitch skipped in the dirt. Derrick fell to his knees to block it but the ball dribbled under him and rolled to the backstop. Jesse ran forward to cover home plate, but he just wasn't fast enough. The runner from third slid into home, scoring on Jesse's wild pitch.

Jesse was shaken. He walked the next two batters. Then Coach Lanigan strolled out to the mound.

"Jesse, I'm going to give you a rest," Coach said. "Eddie's going to relieve you."

Jesse hung his head low and walked back to the bench. He didn't feel like talking to anyone. He couldn't believe how badly he had pitched—or how good Eddie looked warming up.

Eddie was coming into a tight situation. The bases were loaded with no outs. Still, he looked confident on the mound. He started off with a fastball that the umpire called a strike. Next he threw a perfect changeup, and the batter swung way too early, for strike two. Next Eddie pitched a curve, struck out the man, and the Panther bench went crazy.

"All right Eddie!" they yelled. "Let's see some more! There's no way those guys can hit your stuff!"

Jesse didn't join in the cheering. He was too mad at himself for having blown his pitching. He had to admit, Eddie was looking better than ever. Eddie didn't have Jesse's power, but he knew how to keep the Williamsport batters guessing. He struck the next two batters out, and that got the Panthers out of the jam.

"Yeah, Eddie!" the team shouted. "Way to save the day!"

Eddie's great pitching had the Panthers psyched. They scored three runs in the next inning, tying the score at five all.

Eddie kept his cool and only gave up one more run to Williamsport. With great pitching behind them, the Alden batting caught fire. They scored two more runs and beat Williamsport, 7–6.

Even though the Panthers had won, Jesse felt

lousy. He had to force himself to go with his friends to Pete's Pizza to celebrate their victory. He sat in a booth with Eddie, Derrick, and Dan Folger, quietly sipping his soda as the other boys bragged about their great pitches, hits, and plays.

"I'm going home now," Jesse said, in the middle of Eddie's story about a great strikeout he had pitched.

He got up without another word and walked out of the pizza parlor. The whole way home, Jesse kicked at stones. *This must be the start of my bad luck,* he thought. *I knew it would catch up with me, sooner or later.*

6

At practice on Monday, Coach Lanigan put Eddie on the mound to pitch batting practice.

"Keep these guys guessing," Coach said to Eddie. "Just like you did to the Williamsport batters."

Pitching batting practice had always been Jesse's job, and Jesse couldn't help feeling angry as he watched Eddie warm up. It seemed like Eddie was stealing all the glory at the mound.

After Coach had started the outfielders' drill, he walked over to the bench and sat down beside Jesse.

"Let's work on your pitching, Jesse," Coach said, putting his hand on Jesse's shoulder. "We have to get you back into top pitching shape."

Coach led Jesse over to the bull pen where Matt Kindel stood, wearing catcher's gear.

"Why didn't you pitch what Derrick told you to pitch against Williamsport?" Coach asked, as he tossed Jesse a ball.

Jesse glanced at the ground and shrugged. "I guess I just didn't feel confident about my curves and changeups."

"Confidence is the most important thing for a pitcher to have," Coach said. "And the only way to be confident is to practice your pitches. So throw your best curveball at Matt."

Jesse stepped up to the rubber and threw a curve. The ball sped right toward Matt's mitt, and then curved sharply to the left.

"Perfect!" Coach said. "See, you know how to throw a curve. You just need to relax in a game situation."

Jesse nodded. He knew Coach was right. He spent all of practice working with Matt on the curve and changeup. After Jesse had pitched ten or so, he caught for Matt—since Matt was slated to start against North Colby on Wednesday. By the end of the practice, Matt and Jesse were sending off-speed pitches over the plate, one after the other.

After practice, Jesse met Derrick and Eddie at Pete's. Derrick and Eddie were sharing a medium pepperoni pizza, and there was only one slice left.

"Who gets the last piece?" Eddie asked. Eddie was small, but he had an amazing appetite.

"I'm stuffed," Derrick said, leaning back and patting his stomach. "It's between you two."

"Let's flip a coin for it," Eddie said. "That way, whoever has the best luck wins."

Jesse took a quarter out of his pocket and flipped it. Eddie called heads. When Jesse took his hand away he saw George Washington looking right up at him.

"I win!" Eddie said, snatching the last piece of pizza from the tray and shoving it into his mouth.

"You seem to be winning everything these days," Jesse muttered.

"Maybe your bad luck is starting," Eddie said.

"Or maybe you just want to steal my position," Jesse said, staring fiercely at Eddie.

"Hey, I'm a shortstop," Eddie said defensively. "I'd rather be playing the infield."

"Then why don't you tell Coach that you don't want

to pitch anymore?" Jesse said, slurping angrily on his drink.

"Because I want our team to win," Eddie answered. "And we sure won't win if Mr. Bad Luck stays on the mound."

"That's enough!" Derrick cried, holding his hand up to quiet them. "You guys are on the same team, remember? We have to play together if we want to win."

Derrick was right. It didn't do any good for Jesse to get mad at Eddie. Eddie was just doing what Coach told him to do. But still, Jesse wondered why Eddie had to get all the glory.

North Colby was one of the best teams in the league. They had a few big power hitters who had been taking the league apart. North Colby had won their last three games by over seven runs.

Alden had great hitting, too. John Lilly was batting .400—with two triples—Derrick was batting .350, and Dan Folger was batting .340. Eddie wasn't a power hitter, but he could punch the ball right over the infielders' heads for singles. Jesse was having a good year at the plate too, boasting an average of .315.

The game between Alden and North Colby was another battle of the bats.

Matt started the game, and pitched well. After the fourth inning, the score was tied 4–4. In the fifth inning Matt got tired and started making dumb mistakes. He gave up three singles in a row, and Colby chalked up another run to take the lead. He walked the next batter to load up the bases—and that's when Coach Lanigan jogged out to the mound.

Jesse got the nod, and strolled out to the mound to warm up. His curve and changeup felt great as he threw his practice pitches. He looked over at the crowd gathered to watch and saw Nick Wilkerson. He wanted to prove that he was the Panthers' best pitcher.

I just hope my bad luck is over, he thought, touching the baseball card in his cap.

North Colby's biggest hitter stepped up to the plate. He looked like a bear, with big arms and a thick neck. Jesse had a feeling the batter was going to be gunning for a grand slam. He swallowed hard and looked for the signal from Derrick.

Curveball.

Jesse took a deep breath and pitched. The curve bounced into the dirt for a ball. Derrick called for a changeup, and Jesse sailed the next one high. Finally, Derrick gave him the signal for the fastball. Jesse wound up and hurled the ball as fast as he could—so fast that he pulled it high again, for ball three.

Oh, no, he thought. *I can't walk in a run!*

This time Derrick called for a curveball. Jesse tossed it high for ball four. Jesse watched the batter walk to first and the runner on third stroll across the plate for a run.

He felt his confidence crash to the ground. He walked a second runner across the plate, pitching fastballs and curves way out of the strike zone. When the third runner walked across the plate, Coach jogged out to the mound.

"You can head back to the bench, Jesse," Coach said. "Sit down and shake it off. You'll get them next time."

Jesse walked to the bench with his head down and took a seat way over by the water cooler. He couldn't believe that he had just walked three batters. He felt like disappearing and never coming back.

Coach called on Eddie to pitch out of a very difficult situation—bases loaded, no outs. Eddie looked calm, just like he was pitching in Jesse's backyard. He struck out the first batter, then the second, throwing them off with his varied pitches. The third batter grounded to Dan Folger, who touched third base for a force-out.

When Eddie got back to the bench, he was swarmed by his teammates.

"Great pitching!" they cried. "You really got us out of a jam!"

Jesse didn't join in the congratulations. He sat with his head down all alone, over by the water fountain.

The Panthers had a great rally in the next inning. Derrick stepped up to the plate with two down, and men on first and third. Jesse heard the crack of the bat and looked up to see Derrick's hit go sailing way over the left fielder's head. Derrick sped all the way around second, and Coach gave him the signal to round third and go for home.

It was going to be a close play. The left fielder relayed the ball to the second baseman, who whipped the ball toward the catcher. Derrick dove headfirst toward the plate. The catcher caught the throw just as Derrick cut his legs out from under him. Derrick's hand passed along the plate while the catcher flipped and fell on his back in a huge cloud of dust. The ball went dribbling toward the backstop.

"*Safe!*" the umpire cried, holding his arms out.

The Panther bench went nuts. A three-run homer!

Jesse stood up and started to walk over to the group that was mobbing Derrick. He didn't really feel like joining in, so he just turned around and walked back to the bench. He didn't say a word to anyone.

By the end of the sixth inning—with Eddie pitching—the score was North Colby 8, Alden 7.

Eddie pitched a perfect seventh inning—not a single hit—and the Panthers had three outs to send a man home.

Eddie led off with a double, and then Rich Roberts bunted down the first-base line. The Colby pitcher bare-handed the bunt and flipped it to first—over the first baseman's head! Since Eddie had been running on the pitch, he was already halfway down the third-base line by the time the first baseman got a handle on the ball. He slid into home to tie the game.

Jesse didn't say a word. Nor did he cheer when John Lilly drove in the winning run. He just picked up the bat bag and walked to the locker room alone.

A bunch of Panthers asked Jesse if he wanted to go along to Pete's to celebrate, but Jesse just shook his head. He walked home and went straight up to his room, where he stared at the piece of cardboard that covered his broken window.

"Bad luck," he muttered. "Bad luck."

In school the next day, Jesse failed a math test that he had thought was going to be the easiest in the world. Then, at lunch he spilled chocolate milk all over his pants. Now he was sure his bad luck had started—and that Eddie Peres was taking advantage of it.

7

Two days later, Alden was slated to play against St. Stephen's. Jesse told himself that all he had to do was pitch a great game that day, and his bad luck would disappear. Then he wouldn't have to worry about losing the mound to Eddie.

"I want to win this game," Jesse said, smacking his fist in his glove, "and I want to win it bad." The team was on the bus on the way over to St. Stephen's. Derrick sat beside him.

"You will," Derrick said, nudging Jesse with his elbow. "Get out there and throw your best pitches."

Jesse nodded. "As long as I have my good luck card in my cap, I know I have a chance."

"I wish you'd forget about your broken window, and your math test, and all that bad luck stuff," Derrick said, turning to look out the window at the passing scenery. The town of Cranbrook was in spring bloom. All the trees were green and full.

"Well, I haven't had good luck so far this season," Jesse said, taking off his cap to make sure his good luck card was still there. "Eddie is the one who's had all the good . . ."

Jesse's eyes opened wide in disbelief, and his jaw dropped.

"What's wrong?" Derrick asked.

"My card!" Jesse gasped. "It's gone! Someone took my card!"

Jesse tore open his gym bag and frantically checked through everything. He looked in his jacket pockets and turned his pants pockets inside out. He even felt his tube socks to make sure he hadn't put the card in there.

"Oh, no," he mumbled to himself. "Someone took it!"

"You probably misplaced it," Derrick said, trying to calm Jesse down. "It doesn't matter anyway. You can still pitch great without that card. Remember what Coach always says—pitching is all in your head."

"Well, Coach is wrong," Jesse cried, double-checking his gym bag and looking very worried. "I need that card to win."

"No, you don't!" Derrick shouted.

"Yes, I do!" Jesse shouted right back.

"Then I'll give you another card," Derrick said, "and everything will be okay."

"But it has to be *that* card. No other card can give me good luck." Jesse kicked the seat in frustration. "Who could have taken it?"

The bus pulled into the St. Stephen's parking lot, and the Alden Panthers climbed off. Jesse paced toward the diamond, trying to think where his card might have gone. In a flash, it dawned on him. Eddie had stolen it to give him bad luck. Then, when Jesse screwed up on the mound, Eddie would take over and steal all the glory.

"Eddie!" Jesse cried, stomping forward angrily. He poked Eddie in the shoulder. "Give it back!"

"Give what back?" Eddie said.

"My good luck card!" Jesse cried.

"I don't have it," Eddie answered, looking confused.

"It's not a joke," Jesse said, giving Eddie a little push and walking away. "If I screw up on the mound, it's all your fault."

"I don't have . . ." Eddie began, but Jesse had already stormed away.

Fifteen minutes later, Jesse stepped onto the mound and faced his first St. Stephen's batter. By force of habit, he reached up and touched his cap. This time he didn't feel his card there. How could anyone expect him to pitch without his good luck card, especially when he was trying to fight off a whole season's worth of bad luck?

The St. Stephen's player cocked his bat back and gazed straight into Jesse's eyes. Jesse's knees felt weak.

Derrick called for a fastball. Jesse laid his fingers along the seams and wound up. The pitch was way high, for a ball. Derrick called for a curve next, and Jesse threw it into the dirt. The next two pitches were balls as well. The batter took a slow trot to first base.

I knew it, Jesse thought as the next batter took

his final practice swings and walked to the plate. *I knew I wouldn't be able to pitch.*

He walked the next batter, and then threw a wild pitch to advance the runners. Now there were men on second and third. He was already in a bind, and he hadn't even thrown a single strike!

He threw another wild pitch. The runner at third scored easily. He decided that his next pitch would be in the strike zone—even if he had to lob it in there. So he went into his windup and threw a nice fat sitter. The St. Stephen's batter smashed it over Zack's head for a stand-up double, and the runner at second scored.

When Jesse walked the next batter, Coach Lanigan jogged out to the mound, with Eddie following right behind.

"You're not having a good day," Coach said, patting Jesse on the shoulder. "Why don't you go sit down and cool off."

Jesse's face was red with anger. He threw his glove down onto the mound. "So now you're going to let that *thief* take over!" he cried. "He's trying to make me look bad. He stole my good luck card!"

"That's enough, Jesse," Coach said in a firm voice, pointing to the sideline. "Go have a seat on the bench."

Jesse picked up his glove and stormed over to the bench. He sat alone by the water cooler, sulking. If anyone tried to talk with him, he just shook his head and shrugged. Eddie got the Panthers out of trouble, but no one was very psyched up about it. How could they be, when Jesse was so upset?

The Panther batting went on to take apart the weak St. Stephen's pitching, and all Jesse could do was sit there with his arms crossed, stewing. In the next inning Eddie did well on the mound, mixing up his pitches and confusing the St. Stephen's batters.

In the sixth, Jesse watched Eddie strike out the side, one-two-three. After his last pitch, Eddie ran straight over to the water cooler, where Jesse was sitting.

"Aren't you going to congratulate me?" Eddie said, pouring a cup of water. "I just struck out three in a row."

Jesse turned his head away and didn't answer.

"Oh, so now you're ignoring me," Eddie said, gulping down the water. "If this is about your good luck card, I don't know where it is."

Jesse made a little laughing noise, and kept his head turned away. He didn't believe a word Eddie said. Eddie looked at Jesse, crushed his paper cup, and stomped away.

In the seventh inning, Jesse stood up to get a drink of water. He felt something in his back pocket. His heart dropped as he pulled out his good luck baseball card. He was sure he had checked, but it must have been in that pocket all along. He sat down on the bench, his face burning with embarrassment.

Feeling worse than ever, he put the card back in his pocket and watched Eddie win another game for Alden.

8

"I hear you're starting against Bradley today," Jesse said, dropping his milk carton onto the table where Eddie and Derrick were sitting. "It looks like I'll be riding the pine for the rest of the season."

It was Monday after the St. Stephen's game, and the three friends were in the lunchroom of Alden Junior High. Students were talking, laughing, and shouting, and the sun was streaming in through the tall windows. Jesse pulled up a chair and sent Eddie an angry glance as he sat down.

"I didn't decide to pitch today," Eddie said, taking a gulp of milk. "Coach Lanigan told me I was supposed to start. And anyway, you found your good luck card. That proves I didn't steal it."

"You're still starting today," Jesse said, ripping open his lunch bag. "I was supposed to start today."

"Maybe you'll get to play shortstop," Derrick said, trying to calm Jesse down.

"Fat chance," Jesse remarked. "I'm a pitcher, not a fielder."

"We can work on your pitching after the game," Derrick offered.

"Forget it," Jesse said.

"Why?" Derrick asked. "Don't you want to get out on the mound again?"

Jesse shrugged. He just didn't feel like working on his pitching. He wasn't even so sure he felt like playing baseball anymore, now that Eddie was the star pitcher, and he was a first string bench warmer.

That afternoon, Jesse took his seat on the bench. They were playing at home on the big diamond behind Alden Junior High, where the eighth graders usually practiced. Jesse sat with his chin in his hand, watching Eddie warm up with Derrick. He hoped Nick Wilkerson wouldn't stop by on his way to practice. He didn't want Nick to see him sitting on the bench.

"Why aren't you out there on the mound?" came a voice from behind.

It was Nick, leaning up against the fence and smiling.

Jesse felt himself blush. "I'm taking a rest."

"After you pitched a whole half-inning last week?" Nick teased.

"I guess I need some more work on my curve," Jesse muttered.

"I've watched you practice," Nick said. "Your curve looks great, even better than Eddie's. I think your problem is all in your head."

Jesse shrugged.

My problem is that you jinxed me for a whole season by breaking my bedroom window, he thought.

"You guys have a great record this year, anyway," Nick said, turning to walk away. "If the team wins, that's all that matters. Looks like the game's starting, so I'll see you later."

Nick waved good-bye and jogged away.

A moment later, Eddie threw the opening pitch to Bradley—a strike. Jesse noticed that Eddie went through a little ritual before each pitch, just like he did. First, Eddie tugged at the collar of his good luck

T-shirt. Then he adjusted his cap, checked Derrick for the signal, and pitched.

Eddie went on to retire the side. As the Panthers came up to bat, Jesse thought it would be funny to see how Eddie would pitch if he didn't have his special good luck T-shirt. What if Eddie had as much bad luck as he did, and started walking batter after batter? Then Coach would finally give Jesse the nod, and he could save the day. Jesse would strike out everyone with his perfect curve, his trick changeup, and his blistering fastball. He imagined himself stepping up to the plate and smashing a grand slam homer, sliding headfirst into home plate for the game-winning run.

The roar of the crowd broke Jesse's daydream. He looked up and saw John Lilly round first base and sprint toward second. All the boys on the Panther bench were on their feet, cheering John around the bases—all except Jesse. John made it to third with a headfirst slide, barely beating the tag.

"Come on, Jesse!" Bruce Judge called out, waving for Jesse to stand up and cheer. "What's wrong?"

"Nothing," Jesse answered, staying on the bench. "I just don't feel like cheering."

"Oh," Bruce answered. The smile vanished from Bruce's face. A moment later, he sat down, too.

The next time a Panther got a hit, two other boys didn't stand up from the bench. Jesse's attitude was starting to bring the whole team down.

When the inning was over and the Panthers were running out to the field, Coach walked over to Jesse.

"Jesse," Coach said, in a quiet voice. "I know you're disappointed that you're not out there pitching. But I'm going to give you a chance to pitch a whole game this week, no matter what."

"Really?" Jesse asked. "Against South Colby?"

"No, not South Colby," Coach answered. "Matt's pitching the South Colby game. I think you need a chance to prove yourself in a game where there's not much pressure. You throw great in practice, but when the pressure's on, you lose control of your pitching. So I'm going to set up a scrimmage game on Wednesday against the eighth grade team."

"The eighth grade team?" Jesse asked in disbelief.

"Yeah. How does that sound?"

"Oh, great!" Jesse said. "Just great!"

"Good. Get psyched to pitch against the big boys," Coach said with a smile.

Jesse got a drink of water from the cooler and thought about the scrimmage game. This was his big chance to prove to everyone that he was the Panthers' real pitcher—and his big chance to strike out Nick.

Jesse saw it all happen in his mind's eye—the blazing fastball, Nick's big swing, and the umpire sticking up his thumb and calling, "Strike three!" Nick would tip his hat to Jesse as he walked back to the dugout. Jesse would be a star.

Then Jesse remembered his bad luck, and his spirits drooped. He put his chin in his hand and watched Eddie retire the side.

9

That Wednesday, Jesse watched the eighth grade players make their way down the path from the locker room. His heart began to pound like crazy. He stepped off the mound and took a deep breath.

"What's wrong?" Derrick called out, lifting off his catcher's mask.

"Nothing," Jesse answered. "I'm just sizing up the opponent."

Derrick walked across the grass to Jesse.

"Your pitching looks great today," Derrick began,

flipping the ball to Jesse. The two friends had just spent fifteen minutes warming up Jesse's pitching arm. Jesse had thrown his curves and changeups right into the strike zone, and his fastball was as quick as ever. "You can beat those guys, I know you can. You can even strike out Nick."

"Let me make sure I have my good luck card," Jesse said.

Derrick laughed as he watched Jesse take off his cap and check on the card, for the fifth time that afternoon. Once Jesse had made sure the card was still there, he followed Derrick back to the bench.

"Hey, Jesse," Eddie said, as he arranged the bats in a fan on the dirt. "Good luck today."

"Don't you really want to wish me bad luck?" Jesse said. "Then when I blow the game, you'll be sure to get all the glory on the mound."

"Hey, that's not what I said," Eddie said, his face turning an angry red. "I'd rather be playing short-stop, I don't even like pitching. . . ."

Before Eddie could say another word, Coach Lanigan clapped his hands and called the Panthers to order.

"Okay, Panthers," Coach said. "Remember, this scrimmage is only going to be four innings. That means we have to make every inning count. So get out there on the field, and let's see some hustle. Jesse, stay behind for a second."

All of the first-stringers except Jesse jogged out to their positions on the diamond. When everyone was on the field, Coach looked up from his clipboard and right into Jesse's eyes.

"I've been watching you today, Jesse," Coach began, in a low voice. "Your curves and changeups look sharp. If you throw a bad pitch, that's okay. Just come right back and throw a great pitch. Got it?"

Jesse nodded. Then Coach sent him off to the mound to face the first eighth grade batter.

Sam McCaskill walked to the plate, looked Jesse in the eye, and cocked his bat. Derrick called for a fastball, and Jesse wound up. He sent the pitch blazing toward the inside corner of the plate. Sam connected for a hard ground ball. Eddie jumped into action at shortstop, running toward third base and snagging the grounder backhand. He pulled the ball from his glove, jumped, and hurled it toward first. J. P. kept one foot on the bag, stretching to get the throw. Sam sprinted toward first, stepping on the base a split second after the ball entered the first baseman's glove.

"Out!" the umpire cried.

"Great pitching, Jesse," the infield called out as they threw the ball around the horn. "You're looking hot!" A smile broke out on Jesse's face.

The next hitter was Duane Potter. Jesse pitched a fastball, and Duane connected. The ball shot straight up into the air. Derrick yanked off his catcher's mask. The high pop fly started to drift foul and Derrick followed it all the way—right into the low fence in front of the eighth grade bench. Derrick leaned over the fence and stretched his arm as far as it could go. His mitt was right in Dennis Clements's face. The ball landed in the mitt with a pop!

Derrick smiled and tossed the ball around the horn.

"You got 'em, Jesse," the boys in the infield cried, clapping their hands in their gloves. "They can't hit a thing!"

Nick Wilkerson stepped to the plate and gave Jesse a little smile. He took a few practice swings. Jesse took a deep breath. Derrick showed three fingers for the curveball.

Jesse touched his good luck card, and wound up for the pitch. He snapped his wrist on the delivery and felt the ball float way outside. Derrick tried leaping for it, but the ball bounced in the dirt and hit the backstop.

"Come on, Jesse," Coach called from the bench. "Just throw your stuff."

Derrick called for a changeup, but Jesse decided to throw his fastball. He had had enough of making a fool of himself, trying pitches that didn't get the job done.

The fastball sped right down the middle of the plate, and Nick swung his big bat.

Crack!

Jesse's heart sank as he watched the ball sail high over the outfielders' heads. Nick rounded first, then second, then third base before the ball even got to the relay man. Rich hurled it to the plate, but Nick had already scored for a stand-up homer.

As Nick tossed his helmet to the dirt, he looked at Jesse and smiled.

Jesse gave up three more runs that inning. He refused to pitch his curve and changeup, and just threw his fastball instead. The eighth grade team didn't take long to figure his fastball out. In the third inning they scored two more runs, on a stand-up double from Nick. Jesse felt like crawling into a hole and disappearing, but Coach had promised that he'd finish the game.

When it was the Panthers' turn to bat, Jesse just sat on the bench wishing the game was over.

"Come on, Jesse," Derrick said, sitting down beside him. "It's just a scrimmage game."

Jesse shrugged.

"At least help us cheer on our batters," Derrick said. "We've only gotten two hits the whole game."

"Who cares?" Jesse muttered.

Derrick sighed and shook his head. When it was his turn to bat, he struck out on three pitches. The next batter, John Lilly, took a huge cut and dribbled the ball right back into the pitcher's glove for an easy play at first. The Panthers seemed to be swinging the bat in slow motion.

In the fourth and final inning, the eighth graders chalked up seven runs. If it weren't for an amazing play by Eddie at shortstop, they would have chalked up even more.

The eighth graders were in the middle of their fourth inning rally. Nick had driven in two runs with a double, and he was taking a healthy lead off second base. Eddie was standing at second, in case Jesse wanted to pick Nick off.

As soon as Jesse made a forward motion, Eddie ran back toward the shortstop position. The batter swung on and hit a sharp, one-hop line drive. Eddie made a leaping dive, sticking his hand out as far as it would reach, while Nick took off for third. Eddie snagged the ball on a short hop, rolled over in the dirt, and made a swipe at Nick with his glove—tagging him out on the thigh. Then he rose to his knees and sidearmed the ball to first base. J. P. stretched as far as he could, keeping one toe on the base. The ball beat the runner by a hair.

It was an incredible double play, but no one seemed to be excited about it. In the bottom of the fourth, the seventh graders were retired three up, three down. The game was over.

Jesse refused to talk to anybody on the way back to the locker rooms. He didn't know if he was angry or embarrassed. All he knew was that he had made a fool of himself, and it was all because of bad luck.

In the locker room the eighth grade boys razzed the seventh grade boys in a good-natured way. Jesse put on his high-top sneakers and snatched his gym bag. He headed for the locker room door, hoping that he wouldn't have to talk to anyone.

Derrick and Eddie stopped him just before he got to the door.

"Hey," Derrick said. "Do you want to go to the Game Place and play a few video games?"

"Forget it," Jesse said. He gave Eddie a cold glance. "Especially if Eddie comes along."

"Hey," Eddie said, standing in front of Jesse. "I've

had about enough of you. Just because you have bad luck and can't pitch a curveball, doesn't mean you have to blame me."

"Oh, yeah?" Jesse said, giving Eddie a little push. "You've been planning this all along. You're happy to see me lose, so you can take over the mound."

"Quit it," Derrick shouted, stepping between them before a fight could break out. "We're all on the same team, remember?"

"I wish we weren't on the same team!" Jesse said, turning his back and storming out of the locker room.

Derrick and Eddie stood in the doorway and watched Jesse disappear down the sidewalk. Everyone on the team had heard what Jesse said, and the locker room was quieter than ever.

"I'm sick and tired of getting the blame for Jesse's bad pitching," Eddie said angrily as he stuffed his uniform into his gym bag.

"And I'm sick and tired of hearing about bad luck and special cards, and all that stuff," Derrick answered.

"What can we do?" Eddie asked.

"I don't know," Derrick said, shrugging. "But we have to do *something*. If Jesse doesn't break out of his pitching slump, we're going to start losing conference games."

10

Jesse could tell that Matt was having a bad day on the mound. It was only the third inning, and already South Colby had scored four runs. He had to admit, it was kind of fun to watch someone else mess up for once. It made sitting on the bench a little more interesting.

"Come on, Matt," the Panther infield called out. "Show your stuff, fire it in there."

There were runners on first and third, no outs, and

Matt was pitching from the stretch. The man on first had stolen a base in the second inning, so everyone was looking for him to steal again.

As soon as Matt released the pitch, the runner at first took off down the baseline. The pitch was wide and Derrick had to leap to his feet to snag it. He pulled the ball from his mitt, then whipped it to Rich Roberts at second base.

The throw was right on target, but Rich missed it and the ball rolled into center field. Derrick yanked off his catcher's mask and threw it on the dirt, to get ready for a play at the plate.

The runner from third took off toward home, while John Lilly ran toward the loose ball in center field. Derrick positioned himself in front of the plate and crouched to get the throw. John bare-handed the ball in center field and chucked it toward home. The ball floated high above Derrick's head. Derrick jumped for it just as the runner slid.

"Safe!" the umpire cried.

The ball hit the backstop and Derrick scrambled to get it.

In the meantime, the other runner was rounding third and heading for home.

"Eddie, Matt, where are you?" Derrick cried, looking for Eddie or Matt to cover home plate. Eddie hustled toward the plate, but couldn't get there in time. The runner was safe.

That brought the score to South Colby 6, Alden 0.

When the inning finally ended, Coach Lanigan said a few words to the Panther bench.

"One of you was supposed to cover home when Derrick was away from the plate," Coach said.

"I know," Eddie said, looking down.

"What's wrong with you guys today?" Coach asked. "Everyone looks like they've lost their spirit. We've already made three errors today. And Matt, you're got to stop walking batters. We're giving the runs away."

It was true that Matt was pitching his worst game of the season, but all of the Panthers seemed to be having bad games, too. If they kept playing like this, Jesse knew they'd never make it to the championships. And right then, Jesse didn't care.

When the inning finally ended, Alden was down by eight.

Derrick walked over to Jesse and poured himself a cup of cold water.

"Why don't you cheer a little bit and help us get out of this hole?" Derrick asked.

"Why should I?" Jesse answered. "It's kind of fun to watch you guys screwing up."

"Do you know why we're screwing up?" Derrick said angrily. "It's because you're being such a jerk."

Derrick threw his cup down and walked over to the bats. Jesse watched him slide the donut weight onto a bat and take his practice swings. A moment later Derrick walked out to the plate. He cocked his bat back and gazed at the pitcher. The pitch was a fastball, low and inside. Derrick took a cut anyway and missed. Strike one. He missed the second pitch as well. When the umpire called the third pitch for strike three, Derrick tossed the bat against the fence and threw his helmet down.

Jesse had never seen Derrick get angry like that, and it made him feel strange. He wondered if his attitude really was bringing the whole team down.

Matt finished the game, and the Panthers ended up losing 8 to 3. After the game, the locker room was the quietest it had ever been. The only sounds came from locker doors banging shut and gym bags being zipped up.

On Tuesday of the next week, Matt pitched against Lincoln, and the Panthers had the same kind of game. Even after Eddie relieved Matt in the fifth inning, the Panthers couldn't pull it together. Jesse sat alone by the water cooler, and Alden lost 8 to 4.

After the Lincoln game, Derrick and Dan Folger went to Pete's and ordered a medium pizza with mushrooms and pepperoni. No one else had felt like coming along, so Derrick and Dan sat alone in a big booth. When the pizza arrived, neither of them felt much like eating.

"What's happening to our team?" Dan wondered, staring at the steaming hot pizza.

"I don't know," Derrick said. "But I think everything would change if we could get Jesse back on the mound."

"Maybe," Dan said. "It's like Jesse quit on us."

"I've been thinking of a plan," Derrick said. "You know how superstitious Jesse is, right?"

"Sure," Dan said.

"Well, what if we could find a way to prove to Jesse that his good luck card is a bunch of nonsense?" Derrick said. "Then he'd see that his pitching doesn't have anything to do with bad luck or good luck."

"That'd be great," Dan agreed. "But how can we do it?"

"Okay," Derrick said, leaning close to Dan. "Here's the plan."

———

That night, Jesse answered the phone. It was Derrick. "We set up a special scrimmage game for Saturday," Derrick said. "We want you to be the starting pitcher."

"Okay," Jesse answered. "But with my luck, you'd be better off using Matt or Eddie."

"We want you, because you're the Panthers' starting pitcher," Derrick said. "You just have to promise one thing."

"What?" Jesse asked.

"You have to promise that you'll give me your good luck card before the game," Derrick said.

"What?" Jesse cried. "If I don't have my card, I don't have a chance of winning!"

"Just promise me," Derrick said. "If you don't pitch well, I'll give it right back to you."

There was a long pause on the phone.

"Okay," Jesse said at last. "Whatever you say. But if I pitch a terrible game, it'll be your fault."

"That's right," Derrick said. "It'll be all my fault."

11

On Saturday afternoon, Jesse rode his bike to the baseball diamond in Danahy Park. He had his glove looped around the handlebars, and his bat slung across his left shoulder. It was a beautiful spring day, and the park was filled with kids playing on the playground, families eating picnics beneath the big oak trees, and people rowing little boats in the pond. Jesse didn't notice much about the day, though. He only had one thing on his mind—figuring out why Derrick wanted him to pitch without his good luck card. As he approached the diamond, his heart skipped a beat. Nick Wilkerson was there.

"Hey, Nick," Jesse said, climbing off his bike and leaning it against the backstop. "What are you doing here?"

"Don't you know? Derrick asked me to get together a scrimmage team of eighth graders," Nick said, tying his cleats. "He told me you were pitching."

"I am," Jesse answered. "But Derrick didn't tell me I was going to be pitching against you guys."

"It's not a big deal," Nick said, standing up and grabbing his aluminum bat. He took a few powerful practice cuts. "It'll be good batting practice for everyone."

Nick punched Jesse playfully in the arm and walked away to meet the other eighth grade players. When Jesse turned around, he saw Derrick and Dan walking toward him, carrying bases and bats.

"Why didn't you tell me we were going to play against the eighth graders?" Jesse asked Derrick. Derrick dumped the bats on the dirt. Dan ran out to put the bases on the infield.

"I wanted it to be a surprise," Derrick said. He put his hand out in front of Jesse. "Now give me your special good luck card."

"Forget it!" Jesse said, backing away. "I need all the luck I can get, if Nick's around."

"You promised," Derrick answered.

Jesse gave his friend a grimace, and then took off his baseball cap. He pulled the plastic-covered card of Roger Clemens from the rim of his cap.

"What are you trying to prove?" Jesse asked as he handed his card to Derrick.

"I'm trying to prove that your pitching slump doesn't have anything to do with good luck or bad luck, or broken windows or bad grades—or even special baseball cards." Derrick slipped the card into his shirt pocket and patted it. "See, if you get out there and pitch really well, then you'll know that you don't need your card at all."

"What if I screw up?" Jesse said. "Remember, you promised I could have my card back if I started screwing up."

"I promise," Derrick said, patting his shirt pocket again. "But you've had your good luck card with you almost every time you've pitched, and it hasn't helped much."

"I know," Jesse said, blushing. "If I don't have it, maybe I'll do even worse."

Just then, Eddie rode up on his bike. As soon as he stopped beside Jesse and Derrick, Jesse turned around and walked away toward the drinking fountain. He didn't want to be around the guy who had stolen his place on the mound.

"I guess Jesse's still mad at me," Eddie said to Derrick, climbing off his bike.

"I guess," Derrick answered. "But if everything works as planned, he won't be mad by the end of the game."

A minute later, Eddie and Rich Roberts walked over to Jesse. Jesse was sitting by himself at the end of the bench. Rich slapped Jesse on the back with his baseball glove.

"You're going to do great today, Jesse," Rich said. "Your curve has been perfect in practice the last couple of days."

"Yeah, and you've still got the best fastball in the league," Eddie added.

"Hey, Eddie," Jesse said. "Are you wearing your lucky T-shirt?"

Eddie nodded.

"Well, why don't you take it off?" Jesse said. "If I'm supposed to pitch without my card, then you should play without your T-shirt."

Eddie hesitated a moment, unsure what to do. Then he unbuttoned his jersey, and pulled off the ragged white T-shirt underneath. He folded the T-shirt carefully on the bench, and then buttoned up his jersey once again.

"Now we're equal," Jesse said.

Soon, all the boys on both teams were there. Dan Folger's father had agreed to come along and act as umpire.

Jesse walked to the mound, feeling confident. The whole team really seemed to be behind him today. He was almost looking forward to pitching his curve and changeup, just so he could show the eighth graders—and Nick Wilkerson in particular—what he was made of.

The first batter was Sam McCaskill. Derrick squatted down behind Sam and flashed Jesse one finger, for a fastball.

Jesse started to touch his cap. Then he remembered that his card wasn't there. A cold sweat broke out on his brow.

He wound up and delivered a fastball. It skidded in the dirt. Derrick called for a curveball next. Jesse bounced it off the plate and into the backstop.

Sam connected on the next pitch and hit a hard grounder between second and third. Eddie dove toward third, snagging the ball in his glove. He jumped to his feet and whipped the ball toward first, but Sam had already touched the base.

That was the start of the eighth grade rally. Jesse walked the next two batters, and then Nick was at the plate. Jesse wound up and pitched.

Crack!

The ball flew high over John Lilly's head. One, two, three runs were quickly scored, and soon Nick was pumping his arms and rounding third. Derrick stood in front of the plate with his mask off, waiting to get the throw from the cutoff man. The ball flew into Derrick's mitt just as Nick made a perfect slide into home, knocking Derrick down.

Mr. Folger lifted his thumb to call Nick out. Then he saw the ball rolling across the dirt.

"Safe, safe!" he cried. "A grand slam homer!"

Jesse's spirits sank.

The next batter hit a blistering line drive toward second base. Rich Roberts dove and snagged it for the first out. Jesse walked two more batters, but then Sam McCaskill, the eighth grade pitcher, hit into a double play to retire the side. After half an inning, the seventh graders were already down by four.

Jesse finally walked up to Derrick and demanded his card back.

"See, I told you I'd screw up without my card," Jesse said, holding his hand out. "Unless you want to lose by twenty runs, you'd better give it back."

"Why don't you just try another inning?" Derrick suggested.

"No way," Jesse answered. "Give it back."

"Okay, okay," Derrick said.

Derrick reached into his shirt pocket and pulled out the card. Jesse snatched it out of his hand and put it in his cap.

"If I start pitching well next inning, then you'll believe me about my lucky card?" Jesse said.

"If you pitch well next inning," Derrick said with a smile, "then I'll believe anything."

The seventh graders had a good first at bat. Jesse led off with a sharp ground ball that just made it under the second baseman's glove for a single. Rich Roberts struck out, and then Eddie singled into center field, advancing Jesse to second base.

Derrick was next at bat. He hit a deep fly ball to right field. Jesse watched the right fielder run back and back. He stayed with his foot on second, so he could tag up if the right fielder caught the ball. With his slow running speed, he knew that it would be a close play at third, but he was feeling much better with his good luck card in his cap.

As soon as the ball hit the right fielder's glove, Jesse took off toward third. The right fielder was so deep that he had to throw to a cutoff man. The cutoff man chucked the ball to the third baseman. Jesse could hear the cheers of his team as he curled his right leg under, dropped, and went into a smooth slide. He heard the slap of the ball hitting the third baseman's glove, and then felt his foot hit the base. A split second later, the third baseman made the tag.

"Safe!" everyone cried.

In the meantime, Eddie had snuck over to second base. Now the Panthers had two runners in scoring position.

Jesse stood up, smiling. He touched the card in his cap. All his good luck was coming back.

By the time the inning was over, the seventh grade boys had racked up two runs.

The next inning, Jesse felt in control, as he walked out to the mound. He touched the card in his cap, then licked his fingers and wiped them off on his pants. He couldn't wait to face the first batter.

Derrick called for a curve, and Jesse snapped his wrist on the delivery. The ball sped toward the strike zone and dropped to the right, while the batter took a big cut for strike one. Derrick tossed the ball back to Jesse with a smile, and gave him a big thumbs-up.

Derrick called for the changeup next. Jesse kept

his wrist locked through the delivery. The ball seemed to hang in the air, and the batter's timing was thrown off. He swung and missed. Strike two.

Next, Derrick called for the fastball. Jesse blazed one right into the inside corner. The batter swung again and missed again. Strike three!

"Great stuff, Jesse! Way to go! Let's see some more!" the infielders shouted as they tossed the ball around the horn.

Jesse struck out the next two batters in a row.

Everyone congratulated him in the Panthers' dugout, patting him on the back and giving him high fives. Jesse could feel the spirit of the Panthers going higher and higher. This sure beat sitting on the bench and watching the Panthers lose!

"See what I mean about my card?" Jesse said to Derrick. "Now my pitching's hot."

Suddenly Derrick broke into a huge grin.

"What's so funny?" Jesse asked.

"Take a look at your card," Derrick said.

Jesse took off his cap and pulled out his plastic-coated card. He couldn't believe his eyes. It wasn't his good luck card at all. It was a picture of Jesse!

Jesse's mouth dropped open. "What . . . ?"

"I took an old baseball card from my collection and I glued your picture right onto it," Derrick said, laughing. "Then I covered it in plastic just like your good luck card so you wouldn't notice the difference."

Jesse didn't know what to say. He handed the card back to Derrick, thinking hard about all his luck—good and bad—that season.

"I guess this means you want your real card back," Derrick said, taking the Roger Clemens card from his pocket.

"No," Jesse said slowly, smiling a little. "I don't need that card anymore." He turned around to face the rest of the team and clapped his hands. "Let's go, Panthers. Let's show those eighth graders what we can do!"

The whole team came to life. They scored two more runs that inning, to tie the score at 4.

The next inning the first batter Jesse faced was Nick Wilkerson. This time Jesse was ready. He had never wanted to pitch so much in his life. Nick looked a little cocky as he took his practice swings, and Jesse smiled to himself. Derrick called for a curveball.

"See what you can do with this one, Nick," Jesse said to himself. He turned his foot on the rubber and hurled. The ball broke sharply, and Nick took a big swing. Strike one.

Derrick called for another curve, and Jesse threw

a second perfect pitch. Nick swung and missed again. Strike two. Suddenly Nick didn't look so cocky. In fact, he looked a little worried as he gazed at Jesse on the mound.

Next, Derrick called for a fastball. Since Nick was looking for another curve, he swung way too late. The fastball smacked into Derrick's mitt for strike three!

"Yes!" Jesse yelled, throwing his fist in the air. He had finally struck out Nick Wilkerson!

Nick walked off the field, and tipped his hat to Jesse. Jesse tipped his hat right back.

Jesse gave up two hits for the rest of the game, and when it was over the seventh graders had won 6 to 4. Eddie walked up to Jesse and put his hand out for Jesse to slap.

"You're the real pitcher for the Panthers," Eddie said. "Nice game."

"Thanks," Jesse answered. He smiled and slapped Eddie's hand. "I'm sorry about being sore at you. Let's go to Pete's. I'll buy you a pizza."

"I'll buy you a pizza," Eddie said, with a happy grin. "You're the star of the game."

Ten minutes later, Jesse, Eddie, Derrick, and Dan were sitting in a big booth at Pete's. When their large pizza came, Eddie realized that he had left something at the ball field.

"I forgot my special T-shirt," Eddie said. For a moment he looked horrified.

"I forgot my good luck baseball card, too," Jesse remembered suddenly.

They looked at each other a moment, then shrugged and burst out laughing.

"Who needs them, anyway?" they both said, stuffing more pizza into their mouths.

12

On Monday, the Panthers faced Williamsport at home. It was the third to last game of the season, and one of the most important games for the Panthers. If they won, they still had a chance to reach the championships. If they lost, they had to hope that their big rival—North Colby—lost two games before the end of the season. The way North Colby had been playing recently, they seemed unbeatable.

Matt was slated to start against Williamsport. Jesse wished he could start, so he could show Coach

Lanigan how well he could really play. Still, he knew that the scrimmage against the eighth graders had been just that—a scrimmage. He still hadn't proved that he could throw his off-speed pitches under the pressure of a real game.

Still, Jesse's—and Panther—spirit was high as they hit the field that afternoon.

"I can tell that this team wants to win," Coach Lanigan said. He was standing in front of the bench, pacing up and down with his clipboard in his hand. "I don't know what happened over the weekend, but this looks like a different team. You know how important this is. So let's get out there, and keep up the spirit."

Williamsport had strong hitting, and Matt got into trouble early on. After the first four batters, Williamsport had men at first and third, with one run and only one out. Matt pitched to the cleanup hitter and he cracked one into deep right field. Zack turned and ran back, looking over his shoulder like a wide receiver. He made a beautiful running catch.

With two down, Matt pitched a nice fastball and the batter hit a high pop fly into foul territory. Derrick yanked his catcher's mask off and ran toward the Alden bench, looking straight up into the sky. Everyone on the bench was standing because the ball looked like it was going to land right on top of them. Derrick made a leap into the bench and caught it, landing right on top of Jesse and knocking him to the dirt.

"Hey, this isn't hockey," Jesse joked as they climbed up off the ground. "But that sure was a nice hip check."

Thanks to Derrick's great play, Alden got out of the inning down by only one run.

The Williamsport pitcher was hot, and the Panthers didn't even get a hit in their first at bat. Jesse sat on the bench, itching to get out on the mound.

Matt pitched well for the first four innings, even though the Panthers were down 4–2. In the fifth inning, he seemed to lose control of his pitching. He walked the first two batters, and then pitched for a single, to load the bases.

Coach walked out to the mound, and Jesse's heart began to pound. But Coach called on Eddie, and Eddie jogged over to the mound from shortstop. Jesse slapped his leg in frustration. He watched Coach, Derrick, Matt, and Eddie having a conference on the mound. A moment later, Eddie ran back toward shortstop and Matt and Coach walked back toward the bench.

"Jesse, go warm up," Coach said. "I was going to

put Eddie in, but he said he'd rather have you pitching. Get out there and show them your stuff."

Jesse nodded and jogged out to the mound.

It was a hard situation, with bases loaded and no outs. Derrick called for a curve and Jesse started from the stretch. He felt his arm tighten up at the delivery. The ball skidded in the dirt and bounced past Derrick.

The runner on third was advancing on the wild pitch. Jesse ran toward the plate to tag him out. It was a race to the plate. Derrick scrambled to the backstop, picked up the ball, and flipped it to Jesse, who was still running. The base runner slid toward home and Jesse laid the tag right across his shins.

"You're out!" the umpire called.

The Alden bench went crazy. Jesse had turned a bad mistake into a great play. Before the next pitch, Derrick ran out to the mound.

"Just relax, Jesse," Derrick said. "Pretend that this is the scrimmage game against the eighth graders. I know you can do it. Let's try another curveball."

Jesse nodded. When Derrick had settled in behind the plate, Jesse started his motion from the stretch. The curve was perfect! The batter swung and missed! Next, Jesse pitched a fastball. The batter smacked in a line drive toward third. Dan Folger jumped toward the foul line, made a perfect midair catch, and landed on third base. Since the runner at third was leading off, he had been caught off guard. By landing on third base, Dan had forced the runner out for an incredible double play.

Everyone mobbed Dan as they walked back toward the dugout. Alden's great fielding had saved the inning.

The Panther bats caught fire that inning, too. By the top of the seventh, the score was tied at 4.

Jesse pitched a good last inning. He felt confident in his pitches, even though he walked two men. He also struck out one, and forced another to hit an easy grounder. There were men on first and third, and two down.

The pressure was on. If Jesse could retire the side now, the Panthers would only have to score one run to win the game.

Jesse pitched a changeup and the Williamsport batter read it like a book. He took a cut and the ball went floating above Eddie's head at shortstop. Jesse's heart sank. It looked like the ball would drop in for an easy single, and score the runner at third.

Eddie turned and made a last-ditch dive toward the ball, skidding along the grass on his stomach.

He did a somersault and landed on his rear end. When he opened his glove, the ball was there! Eddie held the ball up like a trophy and ran toward the bench.

"Eddie, you saved me out there," Jesse said as he swung his bat. "Thanks a million."

"No problem," Eddie said. "Let's just make sure we score a run this inning."

Jesse led off the inning with a nice single into left field. Eddie struck out, and so did Rich Roberts.

Derrick stepped up to the plate with two down, and Jesse on first. All they needed was one run to win. Derrick took a big cut for strike one, and Jesse could tell that he was swinging for the big hit. Derrick took another big whiff at the second pitch, to fall behind 0 and 2 in the count.

The whole game came down to this pitch.

The changeup hung in the air. Derrick smashed it deep into center field.

Since there were two outs, Jesse was running on anything. He knew he wasn't the fastest member of the Panthers, but he made his legs go as fast as he could. He looked up and saw Coach waving him on.

Jesse rounded third and headed for home. The throw from left field would be coming in soon, so he got himself ready for the slide. He dove headfirst toward the plate just as the catcher snagged the ball. Jesse knocked the catcher so hard that he bobbled the ball. He slid in safe!

They had won the game.

"You men played a great game today," Coach said in the locker room later that afternoon. "You played with real team spirit. Everyone contributed something to the victory. Now let's keep this momentum going right on to the championship."

The whole team let out a big cheer.

"Hey, thanks for telling Coach that you wanted me to pitch," Jesse said to Eddie as they headed out to Pete's to celebrate.

"No problem," Eddie said. "I knew you'd pitch great."

No matter what Eddie said, Jesse knew that he had pitched a good game, but not a great one. It was really the Panthers' great fielding that had saved the afternoon. Still, he had thrown his pitches with confidence.

And he knew that he would be even more confident for the next game.

13

If the Panthers won the last two games of the season, they would win a place in the championships.

Matt pitched the first game, against the weak St. Stephen's team, and won an easy 6–1 victory. Jesse was glad he didn't have to relieve Matt. He wanted to keep his arm fresh and strong for the North Colby game. North Colby was tied with Lincoln for the best record in the conference. Alden was in second place. Since they beat North Colby earlier in the season

Alden would advance to the championship with a win today. Jesse was slated to pitch the big game.

"You proved yourself against Williamsport last week," Derrick said as they rode in the bus to North Colby. "You showed everyone that you can pitch under pressure."

"I don't know," Jesse answered. He was gazing out the window, watching the homes of Cranbrook flash by. "Our fielding won that game. They got a bunch of hits off me."

"We know you can do it," Eddie said, leaning over the seat from behind. "And Coach does too. That's why he wants you to pitch."

"I'm going to give it my best," Jesse said.

Still, he was nervous. He had never pitched under this kind of pressure before, and he hoped he could pull through with good curves and changeups. He remembered what Coach Lanigan had said at the start of the season—baseball is 75 percent pitching. That meant that the whole game—and Alden's chance to make it to the championships—rested on Jesse's shoulders.

Jesse was leadoff batter. He was standing in the on-deck circle with his blue batting helmet on, taking a few last swings with his favorite wooden bat. When Jesse saw Coach walking out, he knocked the donut weight from the bat and took another swing.

"Jesse," Coach began, putting his hands on Jesse's shoulders. "This is a big game. I know you'll do well. Just remember to mix up your pitches and keep your cool."

Jesse nodded.

"Good," Coach said, knocking him on the helmet to wish him good luck. "Now get up there and swing away."

Jesse walked to the plate, took a few practice swings. Then he cocked the bat behind his head. His heart was pounding as the pitcher began his windup and delivery. The ball came right toward the strike zone. Jesse began his swing but at the last moment, the ball curved in and hit the bat. The vibration of the wood sent a painful shock through Jesse's hands. The ball dribbled right up the first-base line, just like a bunt.

"Dig, Jesse, dig!" Coach called from the first base coaching box.

Jesse took off running as the pitcher charged toward him to get the ball. For a split second, Jesse wished he were Eddie. If he had Eddie's speed, he might have stood a chance of beating the throw to first. With his flat-footed gait, Jesse didn't have much of a chance.

"Out!" the umpire called when the ball hit the first baseman's glove.

"Watch out for the curveball," Jesse said to the guys on the bench, as he tossed his batting helmet to the dirt. "It really jams you."

The Panthers didn't score any runs that inning, and Jesse trotted out to the mound.

Before the first batter came up, J. P. threw warm-up grounders to everyone in the infield. Between pitches, Jesse watched the infield practice, and hoped that they were in good form. It was the great Alden fielding that had saved him in the last game, and he was counting on his fielders to pull through for him today.

Jesse pitched a great first inning, striking out one, walking one, and forcing the next batter to hit an easy grounder to Eddie at shortstop. Eddie handled it like a pro, tossing it to Rich at second, who threw it straight into J. P.'s mitt at first base, for a neat double play.

"Nice play," Jesse said to Eddie as they ran off the field.

"Nice pitching," Eddie said. "Your curve looks great."

The only problem with the inning was that Jesse had thrown a lot of pitches. Two of the batters had fouled off six or seven pitches each. As he sat down on the bench, Jesse felt like he had pitched three innings instead of one. He knew that if the game kept up like that, his arm wouldn't have much strength left by the fifth inning.

The Panther bats came to life in the top of the second inning. J. P. was at the plate, and Zack was taking a big lead at second base. J. P. swung on a high pitch and hit a blooper into shallow right field. Zack took off. The whole Panther bench stood up and watched the ball. If the right fielder caught the ball, there was no way Zack could make it back to second base before being forced out.

"Drop, drop!" Jesse shouted.

The right fielder took a dive and missed the ball! The Panther bench started calling Zack in for a run. Zack rounded third and started toward home, while the right fielder was still scrambling. His throw was perfect, but Zack made a headfirst slide right under the catcher's tag. The Panthers were ahead by one.

The rest of the inning went well for the Panthers. Jesse hit a perfect sacrifice fly to bat in a run. When the inning was over the Panthers were up by three.

When the sixth inning started, the score was still Alden 3, North Colby 0. Jesse shook his arm as he walked out to the mound. His shoulder was getting sore, and he wondered if he would really be able to finish the game.

As the inning went on, Jesse felt himself losing control of his pitches. He walked the first batter, and then hit the next batter with a wild pitch to put men on first and second. If he could just jam the next batter and force him to hit a ground ball in the infield, then he could count on the Panther fielding to get him a double play.

Derrick called for a changeup and Jesse pitched it high over Derrick's head. Jesse slapped his glove against his leg and watched the runners advance on the wild pitch. Next, Derrick called for a curve. Jesse didn't think he had enough control to pitch his curve, so he threw a fastball instead.

Crack!

Jesse watched the ball drop deep in the outfield, between left and center. The two base runners scored, and Eddie missed the tag at second.

The pressure was on, and Jesse's arm was feeling more tired than ever. The Colby batters caught on to Jesse's fastball, and started smacking hit after hit. Soon the scoreboard read North Colby 4, Alden 3. The bases were loaded, with only one out. Coach jogged out to the mound.

"Just relax out there, Jesse," Coach told him.

"Take a deep breath. Your pitching has been strong all day. Don't let them psych you out."

"Coach," Jesse said. "Can Eddie finish the game?"

"Why?" Coach said, surprised that Jesse didn't want the chance to finish such an important game.

"My arm is getting tired," Jesse answered.

"Okay," Coach said, giving Jesse a smile. "If you really think so."

Jesse nodded, and Coach called Eddie to the mound.

The Panthers congratulated Jesse as he walked off the field, but Jesse couldn't hide his disappointment. He wished he could have finished the game and—just for once—gotten all the glory himself. Instead he had lost his confidence in his curve and changeup, and pitched his team into a big hole.

It was Eddie's day again. Eddie struck out the next two batters to retire the side, and then led off a Panther hitting rally in the top of the seventh. When the Panthers took the field for the last time, they were ahead by a run. If they kept North Colby at bay for three more outs, they would win the game.

Jesse led the cheering from the bench. He cheered when Eddie struck out the first batter, and he cheered when Dan caught a line drive at third for the second out.

Jesse stopped cheering when Colby's best hitter stepped to the plate, took a big cut, and sent the ball sailing high over John Lilly's head in center field. John turned and ran back as fast as he could, but there was no way he could make the catch. The runner was already on his way to second base by the time the ball hit the ground. Rich ran into shallow center to get the cutoff throw, and Derrick prepared himself for a play at the plate.

The runner rounded third just as Rich got the cutoff. Rich pulled the ball from his glove, and hurled it toward home. The throw was wide and Derrick had to jump toward first base to snag it. He brought his mitt down as fast as he could, just as the Colby player slid. Jesse couldn't tell what had happened next, because a cloud of dust rose up from the plate. The whole season rode on the umpire's call, and it seemed like he took forever to decide.

The runner was out. Jesse jumped, screamed, and ran right over to Eddie on the mound. He gave Eddie a bear hug. A second later, there was a huge mob of blue and gold uniforms on the mound.

The Panthers were going to the championships!

14

On the night before the championship game, Jesse was finishing up his homework when he heard something tap against his window. He walked over, looked outside, but couldn't see anything in the blackness. There was a new, clean pane of glass where the old broken pane had been replaced. Just as he turned to go back to his desk, Jesse heard one of his window panes shatter. A rock fell to the floor amid a pile of broken glass.

Jesse spun around, his heart racing. He put on his

high-top sneakers and walked to the smashed window.

"Who is it?" Jesse whispered, not wanting his parents to hear.

"It's me! Nick!" came a voice from below. "Did I break your window?"

"Yes," Jesse said, half-angry and half-laughing. "Wait a second and I'll come downstairs."

Jesse ran downstairs and out the back door. Nick was standing there with Sam McCaskill.

"What are you guys doing?" Jesse asked.

"Sorry about your window. Boy, am I. I'm still paying for the last one out of my allowance," Nick said. "I hope this doesn't give you bad luck for the championship against Lincoln tomorrow."

"Forget it," Jesse said. "It doesn't mean a thing. You can break all the windows in my house, if you want to."

"Well, we just came over to wish you good luck in the game tomorrow. We'll be in the stands, cheering you on," Nick said.

"Yeah, good luck," Sam said.

"I still want a rematch with you this summer," Nick said. "I can't believe you struck me out in that scrimmage game."

"I struck you out then, and I'll strike you out again," Jesse said, smiling.

"We'll see about that," Nick said, turning to run back to his house. "Just pull off a win tomorrow."

Sam ran off after Nick.

"Hey!" Jesse called. "What about the window?" But the boys had already vanished into the night.

The next day was bright and sunny, and the baseball field at Alden Junior High was in perfect shape. The grass was newly cut, and the infield had been sprinkled with water and raked. Jesse's stomach was tied into knots as he pitched his warmups with Derrick. He knew he couldn't let the Lincoln batters hit a lot of foul balls. His arm would get tired out, and he'd lose control of his pitches.

This time Jesse planned to stay on top of every batter. If a batter started fouling balls, Jesse planned to take a deep breath and throw the best curve, changeup, or fastball he could. He had to beat every batter that walked up to the plate.

"Listen up, everyone," Coach said before the game. "This is the big game, and everyone needs to play heads-up ball. Every single play you make, every single pitch you throw, could mean the difference between winning and losing the championship. Okay, Panthers, let's go get 'em!"

The first Lincoln batter got stuck with the count at 3 balls and 2 strikes. He just kept fouling Jesse's pitches off into the stands. Jesse knew that this was exactly what he didn't need.

Derrick called for a fastball, but Jesse shook his head. He wanted to pitch a curve.

He gripped the ball along the seams, wound up, and snapped his wrist down on the delivery. The ball sped in as fast as his fastball, and the batter swung just as the ball broke.

"Strike three!" the umpire cried.

The Alden fans cheered and called out Jesse's name. Jesse felt his confidence grow. The next batter hit an easy grounder to first, and J. P. took care of it.

The third batter connected for a high pop fly. Jesse could tell it was going to be trouble.

"Call it, call it!" he cried, as he watched J. P., Rich, and John Lilly all running at each other with their eyes on the ball.

John Lilly ran right into J. P. and the ball hit John on top of the head. John and J. P. fell while the ball bounced into the air. Rich held out his glove and caught it easily.

The stands went crazy. It was the most amazing thing anyone had ever seen—to catch a ball after it bounced off someone's head!

Jesse ran to the outfield, to see if John and J. P. were injured. Both of the boys got up slowly, but they were fine. John spent the next ten minutes laughing and holding an ice pack on top of his head.

The Panther bench was full of energy and excitement, but they still couldn't seem to get a run. The Lincoln pitcher was having as good a day as Jesse was, and neither team was stroking many hits.

In the top of the seventh, the score was still 0–0. Jesse walked out to the mound, feeling a little tired, but determined to finish the game himself. This was Lincoln's last at bat. If they could keep Lincoln from scoring now, the Panthers only needed one run to become the conference champions.

The Lincoln batters came out fighting, and right off Jesse pitched for two singles. He began to get worried, as the Lincoln players got more and more excited about a rally. Jesse took a deep breath each time and pitched his best pitches. His curveballs were right on target. The next batter went down swinging.

Jesse's arm was starting to feel more and more tired, and he shook it out before every pitch. He even began to lose control of his fastball, and walked the next batter to load the bases. Coach Lanigan walked out to the mound.

"Should I put Eddie in?" Coach asked. "It looks like your arm is getting tired."

"No, Coach," Jesse said. "I can do it."

Coach looked Jesse right in the eye.

"You know how important this is, Jesse," Coach said. "Our whole season is riding on this inning."

"I know," Jesse nodded, shaking his arm. "I can do it, Coach."

Coach gave Jesse a smile, and walked back to the Panther bench.

Since the bases were loaded, Jesse was pitching from the stretch. He tossed a perfect fastball for strike one, and then threw three balls in a row. Derrick ran out to the mound and handed the ball to Jesse.

"We don't want to walk a run in," Derrick said. "Just keep your cool and get the ball over the plate."

Jesse nodded and Derrick jogged back to the plate. Jesse pitched his fastball over the plate. The batter hit a sharp grounder right back at Jesse's feet.

Jesse put his glove down by instinct and caught

the ball. Derrick was standing on home plate and Jesse threw the ball to him for a force-out.

Jesse had made a great clutch play, but he didn't have time to savor it. He had other things on his mind—like how to retire the next Lincoln batter, with the bases loaded and two down.

In his mind's eye, Jesse saw the batter hit a grand slam homer, or a double, or even a single. Any kind of hit would put the Panthers in a bad position.

Jesse pitched himself into a 3–2 count. It seemed like the whole season was coming down to these last few pitches. The bleachers grew very quiet. Jesse's palms began to sweat.

Derrick called for the curveball.

Jesse took a deep breath. He laid his fingers over the seams and got into the stretch position. He stared right into Derrick's mitt, and thought about putting the ball right on target. He pitched. The ball sped toward the strike zone. The Lincoln batter took a big swing just as the ball curved inside at the very last second.

"Strike three!" the umpire called.

Jesse whooped and jumped into the air. Then he ran toward the bench as the crowd let loose a huge round of deafening cheers. Coach Lanigan was there to greet him, wearing a big smile on his face.

"You did it, Jesse!" Coach congratulated him. "You had everyone on the edge of their seats and you did it!"

Now all the Panthers had to do was score one run. Then they would be the conference champions. If they didn't, the game would go into extra innings.

Jesse led off.

"Get out there and give us a hit," Derrick said to Jesse.

"I'm going to smack this one," Jesse said, finishing up his practice swings.

Jesse stepped to the plate and cocked his bat back. He swung on the very first pitch. The sound of a solid hit rang through the air.

Jesse hestitated a fraction of a moment at the plate. He couldn't believe his incredible hit. Derrick and the whole Panther team jumped to their feet, crying, "Run, Jesse, run!"

Jesse took off for first base as the left fielder sprinted toward the weeds at the edge of the woods. The ball dropped thirty feet beyond him. Jesse rounded second base, and went for third. As Jesse rounded third base, the cutoff man caught the ball and turned to throw it home.

The whole Panther team was crowding out of the dugout toward the plate. Jesse hit the dirt and the throw hit the catcher's mitt. Everything was hidden by a cloud of dust—everything except the umpire holding his arms straight out at his sides.

"Safe!"

A second later, Jesse felt himself being lifted off the ground by his teammates. Before they could hoist him onto their shoulders, Jesse grabbed Eddie's and Derrick's arms and raised them in triumph. The other Panthers mobbed them, yelling and cheering.

This time the glory belonged to the whole team.